A
Year in Fife Park

A novella by Quinn Wilde

www.fifepark.com

A Year in Fife Park
First published in Great Britain by Willow Ink, 2010.

First Edition (Fife Park Edition)
© 2000-2010 Quinn Wilde

ISBN: 0-9552269-1-0
ISBN-13: 978-0-9552269-1-5

For Ella

Disclaimer:

I remember absolutely every moment, detail and event written in this book. Sometimes the pacing is uneven. Some chapters are very short. That is because nothing has been altered.

That said, of course, all the characters, events and situations portrayed within this book are entirely fictitious and not based on any real experiences, persons, or places.

Except for Fife Park. That place really did exist, although I may for legal reasons be writing about a different one.

Contents

The Big Three Oh... 1

New Term, New Quinine... 3

Home of Golf.. 5

Upstairs 7

Five of Seven 12

Raspberry Canes, Nineteen Eighty-Six. 17

Surf and Turfed Out 20

Darcy Loch's Whey Pat Flat 27

Thunderballs 34

Moving and Shaking 45

Divan, Divan 48

The Glow 55

The Dark Room... 56

Theme Park 69

Darcy Loch's Pub Golf Hole-in-one...................................... 71

Media Sift 83

Green Themes.. 86

Cassie 94

The War of the Randoms 97

The Crack of McWinslow.. 101

Wallow Man... 107

Constitutional.. 110

The Dudes 120

Beasting.. 130

David Russell Apartments 139

David Russell Hall 141

Smoking Gun 147

The Wood and The Burn 150

The Tortoise and the Hare 155

VolcanoHead 161

Fussball 163

Darcy Loch and the Last Midnight Walk 166

The East Nuke 170

May Dip 174

Post 181

The Big Three Oh

I am a grown man. I have a house, and a well paying job. I am desperately unhappy.

I'm unhappy all of the time, but that doesn't stop me from enjoying myself. If you can't see past that contradiction, you are probably one of the many people who would never guess that I'm unhappy. You probably don't believe me, even now. If you knew me, you'd believe it even less. Thanks a lot. This Oscar-winning performance is for jerks like you.

I am not having a mid-life crisis. I am thirty years old. As it turns out, that is not particularly old, and it doesn't make me unhappy. Just sometimes, I wonder how I spent the last ten years. But this is not an age thing. I'm glad I'm thirty. People take me seriously. At first, anyway.

I bought a house at the worst time in history, because it was the right time for me. I knew it was the worst time in history. Other people said it was the best. I waxed lyrical about it at the time – sometimes, I said, you just have to do what's right for you. It's right for everyone, people said, houses only ever go up in value! Now that the crash has happened, everybody else saw it coming and I'm the idiot. That doesn't make me unhappy. That makes me feel smug and unappreciated. Plus, I like owning my house. I would have paid double to end my hate-hate relationship with estate agents and landlords.

I appear to be good at my job because, frankly, most people are not. They are the smart ones. Being good at your job is an awful idea. You will only ever get extra work by being good at something, and you will be passed over for promotion because you're too damn valuable to lose. That doesn't make me unhappy. That makes me exhausted. If I end up having a breakdown, that *will* make me unhappy, but I expect that by then I'll be too far gone to care.

For a long time I simply had no idea why I was unhappy, and no notion to do anything about it. I thought there was just something wrong with me. But then I remembered that there had been a time when I felt differently. There was a time in my life when I felt happy, all of the time, even when I was miserable. Ten years have passed. Now mostly the feeling I get, when I think back to St. Andrews, is that I have momentarily lost something of great importance.

Sometimes these days I walk from room to room, looking for something I had just seconds ago. And sometimes, doing so, I find it. That's the best explanation I have for what follows.

It will be a mess of memories, as best they are remembered. It will be a scattershot of histories, because I do not know what parts I can afford to leave out. There are mistakes and faux pas, damages and destruction, passions and revelations, longing and belonging, love, mystery, tragedy, respect, and just a tiny little bit of sex which has been romanticised and overstated to the point of hyperbole, and in any case was had by other people.

It can start like this: I spent a year in Fife Park. Nothing at all happened, and nothing ever changed me more.

New Term, New Quinine

Every year in St. Andrews had a different theme; every year had a different feel, a different texture, a different atmosphere. The year in Fife Park, which I will consistently refer to as 'Second Year', was a sophomore journey of borderline psychosis. Only an idiot could be nostalgic about some of the memories I will recount.

I am just such an idiot. I can still recall the élan of those days with a trip through my MP3s folder. Guided by Frank's discerning taste, I still dearly hold on to The Delgados, Belle and Sebastian, six cover versions of Aha's *Take On Me*, and a funny mashup of Star Trek dialogue that makes it sound like Spock is boldly fucking Captain Kirk in the ass.

I was in new territory, all that second year, because I'd been so lost in the first. I'm not proud of the person I used to be. I didn't know much about the world, but I knew just about enough to be a douchebag. I used to blame everyone but myself when my blindnesses caught up with me. I used to scream and wail with entitlement. I used to be a little shit. And I am lucky, so very lucky, that I did not simply grow into the fullness of adulthood without being made aware of that, as most people do.

When I finally caught up with myself, at the end of the first year in St. Andrews, and at the beginning of this book, I was a damn mess. You should know this. I was happy, all of the time, even when I was miserable; it's true. But I was miserable kind of a lot, as well.

I made more mistakes in that first year than I've ever made. So many that it was sometimes impossible to tell where I'd gone wrong, or what to learn from them. I am fortunate to have had friends who were in equal parts forgiving and critical, or else I might have never known.

A lot of Freshers died in that first year. Seven or eight, I think. A few fell off cliffs. One of them was one of us, though I never knew him well enough. There weren't many other years like ours. For one guy, it was at the very beginning of the year, away on an introductory Mountaineering Club field trip, held even before any lectures had begun. His parents were still in town, in fact. I can't imagine anything worse. Then again, some poor chap got hit in the chest with a football and died on the spot. All of which goes to show that you can never tell how things are going to work out.

Home of Golf

I stood in the hallway of Fife Park 7, braced against the screams coming from the kitchen, but not yet braced enough to enter.

'You fucking cunting bitching fuck.' So came the next wave of expletives.

It was followed by a series of crashes, some isolated thumps, an almost comic tinkling of glass, and several further crashes.

'You cunting fucking mothercunting shit fucker!'

My hand hovered over the handle.

'Who's he shouting at?' Mart asked, behind me. 'What's going on?'

'Nothing,' I said. 'It is what it is.'

'Very Zen,' Mart said, unimpressed. 'You should get in there. He might hurt himself.'

I pushed the door, and a spray of porcelain flew past my nose, right to left. It was *my* porcelain. Another mug hit the door before it was half open. I poked my head around the door.

'Hello,' I said.

It wasn't any time for reason. It wasn't any time for smalltalk. Another mug was lightly tossed, and he spun the golf club round to intercept it. I pulled my head back into the hallway just in time.

'Fucking bastarding shiteating cuntbreathing fucking cocksores.'

When you use the word cunt as frequently as an angry Scotsman, it can be hard to find something stronger, for those *special* occasions.

'Cocksores, huh?' Mart said.

'Are you okay in there?' I called through, voice raised and strained - like he'd been in the shower for forty minutes. Another fracturing crash.

'Hello?' Mart shouted after.

I looked in again.

The cupboard doors were off, and three more kicks took out the drawers, bam, bam, and bam. The 7 Iron came down hard on the edge of the work surface.

It cracked, shards flew off. It was chipboard underneath. I shut the door firmly.

'We're going to let him work it out,' I said. 'Whatever it is. I don't care about the kitchen. It's not mine.'

'And the plates?'

'Yes, they're mine. That changes nothing.'

The crashes came for minutes on end. Eventually they slowed, like almost-done popcorn. Mart reached for the door handle.

'Give him a minute,' I said. We gave him two.

Frank emerged from the kitchen. The picture of composure.

'Should have used a six,' he said, tossing me the club.

There was trouble, later.

'If I live to be a thousand, I will never understand this,' said the wrinkled killjoy at Residential Services. She looked like she had just about a year to prove herself right.

'Neither will I,' I told her, honestly. 'It's just shit that happened.'

Upstairs

Fife Park, at the time, was the cheapest student accommodation in the UK[*]. That does not make the final repair bill, which eventually tallied up at significantly more than a year's rent, any less impressive.

The park is a shitty set of early 1970s buildings, modelled on your average pebble-dashed, papier-mâché suburban Scottish council estate. At the time of writing, Fife Park is fast approaching its final year on this earth, and has been around nearly forty years longer than I would have expected it to last in the brisk winds of Fife.

Each house has six bedrooms; three up, three down; two toilets (with one shower between them); a kitchen which can comfortably seat four, as long as nobody is trying to cook; and a hallway, with a flight of stairs. At the top of the flight of stairs is a sheer drop, made 'safe' by a little wooden barrier which cuts off just below the average person's centre of gravity.

The walls are made of painted cardboard. The rooms, and the two miniature corridors separating them, were carpeted in some kind of rough green hair which, barefoot, was oddly painful to walk on. The upstairs toilet was floored with something blue and slightly spongy.

We had the upstairs of Fife Park Seven. I was in Room Five. My partners in crime at the start of that year were Craig McCartney, and Frank McQueen.

---

[*] We paid around twenty-nine pounds per week, a figure which will become less connected to reality with every passing year, until one day I'll simply have to refer to it as 'old money'.

Craig has the physical build of the undead. Tall and broad-shouldered but utterly emaciated, he carries himself with a slight shrug, and arms that suggest they are reaching out towards you, even when at his side; a posture that makes him seem permanently ready to spring.

He's got just a trace of that bad guy streak that women like. This is fundamentally because he is a bad guy. It is also, in part, because he is highly, and deliberately, mysterious. It was no surprise when he announced his mysterious past – in as many words – and then shortly into the year started dating a mysterious girl. Years later, he got a mysterious job. This also came as no surprise, although if the job is anything like the girl, he'd have been better off staying at home and stabbing himself with a fork from nine to five.

Craig once told us he had left Dundee because he killed a man. Anyone can say they killed a man. Some guy called Robin told us he killed a man, one night. We called him Bobby Bullshit for four years on the back of that. We didn't call Craig a damn thing, just in case.

Craig is also capable of the unexpected – or perhaps it would be more fair to say that he never ceases to amaze me. The unexpected was something we both celebrated, back then. We would drink to Random together, and Random would find us. Looking back, I can see how much this meant to me. It is the paradox of the gambler; when something is random, there is hope beyond one's own means. At nineteen, that was probably just the hope that I'd get laid, or at least home. But ten years on, finding myself desperate and hoping for hope itself, I wonder if it would be as easy as raising a glass with a friend, to feel so free again.

I value my friendship with Craig tremendously. At the darkest fringes of myself, he understands me. I wonder sometimes if we are similarly broken in some way. We do not talk about such things, but we joke, casually and confidently, about the worst of human nature. Craig exudes confidence, but does not do many things casually. He is stubborn, uptight, and controlling. He's clean, particular, and demands order. We found a tube of Anusol in the bathroom one day, and he didn't even *pretend* it belonged to anyone else. He held out surprisingly well in Fife Park, all things considered.

Frank McQueen, on the other hand, was a big, hairy man. There's no fairer way to put it. He wore a hooded top back before that was grounds for an ASBO, and wasn't afraid to wear it with the hood up. Frank had a dark and tousled mess of shoulder-length hair, which was as thick and intractable as the very real man-rug poking up through the V of his collar. He owed his style as much to the Unabomber as to Ché Guevara, but the effect was all his own.

'I am the Walrus,' Frank would say. He would say this several times a day. It was unquestionably the case, and a source of great pride.

Frank was a medical student. There are two kinds of medical student in the world, and I've lived with both. On the one hand you have the type who are certain that most things that aren't book shaped are going to kill them, who wash their fruit before eating it and dial Emergency if they swallow a couple too many aspirins in a 24 hour period. They study conscientiously, get early nights, and believe everything they read in textbooks.

And then there's Frank McQueen, somewhere just behind the vanguard of the opposing side; the medics who have realised

9

that the human body is virtually indestructible and that it takes a hell of a lot more than pesticide and bird shit to take the wind out of your sails. They tend to drink, smoke, party on obscure drugs that don't even *have* vernacular names, and crave anything that will push them closer to that little bit of life's speedometer that would usually be coloured in red.

It would be an injustice to call Frank easygoing. When Craig finally snapped and put in his request to move out of Fife Park, the last-straw event he cited was stepping on Frank one night, barefoot with the lights off. Frank, who had passed out face down three feet from the door of his bedroom, was naked. He didn't even stir.

In our First Year, Craig and Frank had lived next to each other in the Pink Prison that is New Hall[*], thrown together by the fates, or by whatever system of assignment the fates had delegated to Residential Services. I don't think any of us realised how little this had prepared them for each other.

The Randoms lived downstairs, in rooms One, Two, and Three. We called them The Randoms, as a collective, even after we had been properly introduced. We called them The Randoms long after they had expressed annoyance with this.

They had all been to school together, and had all elected to live together. They all came from in, or near, the same small and unexalted village of Strathblane. I have since been to Strathblane precisely once, and can confirm that it was most likely founded according to traditional local principles: by

---

[*] I've always thought the official name showed a stunning lack of either optimism or foresight on the part of its constructors. Perhaps they'll rename it when it starts to show its age. If so, I hope they open it to nominations.

hammering together a couple of Scottish-sounding syllables and then building a pub[*].

'Quinn, you know they're all from the same village?' Frank asked me, late the first night. '*Strathblane,* apparently.'

We downloaded Duelling Banjos, and played it with the volume up.

---

[*] Strathblane is just a handful of miles north of Milngavie where, given the dichotomy between spelling and pronunciation, they presumably built the pub first.

Five of Seven

My room was freezing cold, pitch black half the time, and there was usually someone semi-conscious sprawled out on the bed. Often this was me. Despite this, my room was the most popular in the house, not counting the kitchen. This was almost certainly because of my open-door policy, because there were slightly fewer pairs of dirty boxer shorts on the floor than in Frank's room, and because I had the best computer by a country mile.

Craig also had a computer, and quite a good one, but he did *not* operate an open-door policy. In fact, he used to *close* his door and repeatedly lock and then unlock it for fifteen straight minutes, until he was satisfied that it was locked. Then he'd do the same thing with the light switch. From outside the house, it probably looked like he was hosting a very small and lonely rave.

Craig kept his room like a boot camp. Every surface was cleaned and dusted, he used his own crisp linen on the bed, and the room permanently smelled of polish, air freshener, fabric softener, and cologne. We were only rarely granted access. I was actually beaten from the room with a rolled up newspaper for farting on one of the few occasions I managed to infiltrate the citadel.

By contrast, people came and went with my room, and usually I liked that arrangement[*]. For all the time I spent in my bed, there would usually be at least one person sitting at my desk.

---

[*] On the other hand, it smelled of man-sweat and smoke, which I could take or leave.

The computer would always be doing something; if nothing else, it would be playing music. Second year caught Napster on the rise, and so we were never short on tunes[*]. Frank signed up for a Yahoo! ID at the start of the year, which he used to play chess and insult Americans.

That came as something of an epiphany for me. I had always guessed that the vast majority of jerks on the internet were backwards twelve year olds, high functioning morons, puerile incompetents with nothing better to do with their lives than incite petty hate mail and create discord, future night-porters and garage attendants to a last man. In short, the very sort of people who are most unlikely to find themselves studying medicine.

Frank McQueen was an above average chess player, and also an internet jerk extraordinaire. He'd go into teen chat rooms as 'SonOfSaddam', and insult three shades of crap out of anyone who was trying to be nice. He'd get on side with a conversation for a couple of minutes before turning tail, and insulting anyone who agreed with him. If there was a point or reason to any chat room, Frank would argue the opposite, with expletives on top. He even insulted people while he was playing them at chess.

'Good move!' he would say. 'You fucking cunt.'

I cringed with embarrassment at some of the propositions he made in the 'Romance' groups. I hid my head in shame when he infiltrated the 'Book-Lovers' group. And I absolutely could not condone some of the things he said in the Christian chat rooms, but hell if those Christians didn't give as good as they got. Usually minus the swearwords; but not always. I guess that's

---

[*] Original Napster, yo.

what Frank was hoping for and, against all expectations, it was pretty compulsive viewing.

The mid-year implementation of 'voice' chat may have been Yahoo!'s most significant error of judgement. Buying a microphone was mine.

'Dude, are you Irish?' one confused debutante asked, shortly before being subjected to a tirade that might have reduced lesser 'Girl Talk' chatters to tears.

'East Coast,' Frank said, making a gang sign. 'Of Scotland, bitch.'

Pretty soon I signed up for a Yahoo! ID of my own. I made up my name from the side of a bottle of tonic water that was sitting on my desk, and then got down to some abuse of the service. It was liberating enough, but I could never get any conviction into my insults, and it didn't feel like me, so I gave up and started to take it all seriously, instead.

'You are such a fucking jerk,' people would tell Frank.

'I am the Eggman,' Frank would say, if he was feeling mellow. Then he'd light up and put on a few tracks.

Sometimes we'd hear Craig screaming wild obscenities from his room. At first we thought he was getting in on the game, too, but later it turned out that he was generally asleep at the time. Frank started locking his door at night for a while after that came out. Even people who don't give a fuck have limits.

I asked Craig recently why he thought he had been so anal retentive in Fife Park, whether he thought he genuinely had OCD, and whether he thought he'd mellowed out these latter years. He didn't, as it happens. His exact statement, word for word, was:

'If my recollection serves, you were a nut. 100% so. Lived in the dark, died your hair semi ginger, wore the worst clothes, smashed up your guitar, and had strange issues. So... it's all down to interpretation.'

It's hard to argue with that comeback. For one thing, it's all true – so it would be kind of an uphill struggle. For another, he's right - this *is* my interpretation. Who else would I look to? Please understand, I'm not making any great claims to my own mental health, but if it's really all down to interpretation we won't be using Craig as the benchmark for fucking apple-pie ordinary.

True, I did smash up my guitar, but not until much later in the year. Also true, I dyed my hair, with limited success, and this had a lot to do with the guitar getting smashed. But taken out of context, that gives kind of a false impression. It makes it sound like I was being pretentious and post-punk, but actually coming off like an asshole. In fact, I skipped the facade entirely – I was being a straight-up asshole, with no subterfuge. It was an emotional time, and I handled it with my usual aplomb. But I'll get to that.

Guilty as charged on most of the other stuff, as well. The clothes, for example. I was going through kind of a flamboyant phase that I'd nurtured during first year. It wasn't about fitting in with any social group, or any style as such. I didn't ascribe to any ethos regarding dress sense or personal politics, and if I'm honest it's probably because I didn't really know how. I had a lot of half-formed opinions; some of them might even have been interpreted as 'strange issues'.

Unlike Frank, I wasn't out of control because I thought life was more fun that way. I was just one of life's bad drivers, swerving all over the road, desperate to be in control. Fuck, I wasn't thrilled to be all angles at all times. I was happy, but I was frantic. I was happy, but I didn't think things were right. They felt like they were, but I knew that they weren't.

How can I even describe that feeling? I'm looking to get it back; I don't even know what it is. It felt like calm, while I was raging round it.

Craig doesn't think this book tells the truth.

'It's all down to interpretation,' he says.

He must be right, because I think it does.

Raspberry Canes, Nineteen Eighty-Six.

You maybe think I'm a miserable person already, because of how I introduced myself. I'm actually kind of fun most of the time. At least, I hope so. Regardless, I'm pretty easy to entertain. And if the last couple of thousand words haven't clued you in already, I'm pretty easily distracted, as well.

For example, I'm going to talk about something that happened over twenty years ago in this chapter, which even the most patient of us would admit is almost completely unnecessary. On the other hand, I explain things best by points of reference.

Where am I? Literally, right now, I'm thirty, I'm at my desk, in my flat, in Edinburgh, and I'm trying to remember being twenty, because I think there was something worth knowing back then. Something worth feeling, at any rate. You remember how I came in on that? Now, I know what you're thinking, if you're thinking at all, and if you're anything like me.

How do I know that what I am searching for was ever really there?

You're wondering, maybe, if I've deluded myself about the wonderful year I spent in Fife Park. Maybe you've even seen Fife Park for yourself. Maybe, you're thinking, I'm just wearing my rose tinted glasses.

That's a good point. Sometimes, even I'm given to wondering if I was ever really as happy as I remember. After all, it's been a while. And Oscar Wilde famously said that 'Nothing ages like happiness.' What if I'm only remembering the good, and discarding the bad?

I'm quite sure that's partly true. I don't see that as too much of a problem. Good riddance to the shitty times, I say. There were a few of them, after all. But I'm also quite, quite certain that, perhaps against probability, I am not just making something out of nothing. There really was a special feeling to those days that underpinned it all.

How do I know? Because I remember it, sure. But not just because I remember it, but because I have one perfect, unalterable memory of it - and it is a memory which is not subject to the usual distortions and the decay of time. This memory cannot lie, because it is as much a message as a recollection. It was constructed out of purpose.

I have only a handful of such memories across the whole of my life, and they are all special to me.

The first now seems to be almost from a different world. When I was seven years old, I wondered how memories might work. I knew that I did not remember everything, but that important moments were prone to stand out.

Sitting on the low wall near our raspberry garden I felt the setting sun on my back, on my side, and the chill of the early evening pinching lightly at my bare legs. As I balanced on the wall, so I balanced between warmth and cold, day and dusk, aglow with contentedness. It was a beautiful moment, in an ordinary day. But it was a moment I decided to keep.

So I committed to keep that memory forever. I took the moment apart, piece by piece in my mind's eye, and swore to myself that I would remember it for the rest of my life. I made it the most important thing in my mind, and I sat there running it over and over in my head, till I felt like it was burning behind my eyes. I kept it going until long after the moment had passed, until it was nearly dark. But I don't remember the dusk coming on, or how I went inside, or what I did before bed. I remember sitting there, in that moment, warmth on my back, making a message in a bottle, in a mind. And it's funny because, though the time between then and now seems like twenty times forever, I know I am the same person.

I also know how I felt that day. Not just because I remember the feeling, which could have been misinterpreted or glossed over with time. I know how I felt because I remember the process of remembering. I remember what I was trying to say, the message in the memory. I remember what I told myself I would.

So there is the answer, in a roundabout way. I know that I was so perfectly content in St. Andrews, because I told myself so at the time, and I'm almost certain that I wouldn't have lied.

Surf and Turfed Out

Freshers Week in the Second Year came and went almost without incident which, given the flatulent events line-up, you could have been forgiven for thinking was the plan. There was one oddly shining star in the week – an unofficial black-tie ball called the Surf and Turf, which was being openly condemned by the Student's Association. That was the first point in its favour. The second was the venue: in amongst the fronds and fishes at the Sea Life Centre.

The price for admission was pretty steep, but included unlimited cocktails. Craig was up for it, but I couldn't persuade anyone else. I spent all day looking for a pair of formal shoes that would fit my monstrously large feet, and I came up with squat.

'What the hell are you wearing?' Craig asked, when we went to get our taxi.

'Golf shoes,' I said.

'Oh, great. Fucking great. Maybe we'll get a game in on the way home. Way to go, asshole.'

The atmosphere in the Sea Life Centre was perfect. We had pretty much the full run of the place, wandering down dark corridors windowed with fish tanks full of tropical (and sometimes utterly hideous) fish. There were a few rooms large enough for people to mix in, and they had been converted into cramped dance floors. The drinks were free as promised and as freely flowing, at first. The place was on three levels, indoors and outdoors, and was, to put it mildly, sexy as hell. Everybody there was loaded.

There was music pumping throughout, and a live band in one of the bigger areas. We bumped into a couple of the Randoms there and exchanged drunken greetings, even though we couldn't remember each other's names, or hear anything we said over the sound of the music. One of the guitarists broke a string, and carried on playing the song. Occasionally it would get in the way, making a scratchy, amplified rasping sound. It was exactly that sort of an off-the-cuff night.

'This place is alright,' Craig said. This was more praise than I had ever heard Craig use in a single sentence before.

'It really is. The other half are in tonight, eh? I hardly recognise anyone[*].'

'They don't stay at the Park, Quinn, that's for sure.'

'Where do the fuck *do* they stay?'

'Sallies. And big fuck-off penthouse flats hidden in the middle of town.'

'No regrets on that front?' It seemed like the right time to ask.

'I spent a lot of time in Fife Park last year, too,' he said.

'Yeah, but mostly, she came out to yours at night.'

'Mostly,' he said.

'Cause Fife Park is shite.'

'Yeah. God, it's fucking awful.'

'You think all this music is bad for the fish?'

---

[*] In St. Andrews there are only two explanations for not immediately recognising everyone within a hundred yards, and one of them is amnesia. The other is that you've stumbled head first into the old boy's network.

21

A bright yellow and blue fish in a nearby tank seemed to be swimming in time with the band. It was upside down.

'Doubt it. They'd never have hired the place out, if it was[*].'

'I'm amazed they did. This place is unreal.'

'Cocktails are pretty low rent, though,' Craig said, swirling his plastic beaker[†].

'Listen, Craig,' I said. 'This year's going to be different.'

'Yeah,' he said. 'Potentially.'

'We're off to a good start,' I said.

'Best start ever.'

'But I meant me,' I said. 'It's going to be different this year.'

'Okay.'

'I'm going to sort it all out, mate,' I said. 'All of it.'

He shrugged, honestly.

'Quinn, you think some things are important that aren't. You don't get what's important to everyone else. You're a total fuckup.'

'I've got my issues,' I relented, cheerfully.

'Mate, everyone has issues, but yours don't make any *sense*.'

'Look, I've got a plan,' I told him. 'I know what I need to do.'

I expected him to be interested. He wasn't.

---

[*] Later we found out that what was really bad for the fish was the sheer number of assholes emptying their cocktail glasses into the tanks.

[†] Colour by Dettol, flavour by blue Ice Pop. Or possibly the other way around.

'You know, you're a lot more fun when you're not getting obsessed over some shit that doesn't mean anything.'

'Yeah, maybe,' I said.

There was a wooden veranda outside which looked out over the half lit bay, and a barbecue setup with hotdogs and snacks. Craig disappeared at some point, and I was left standing alone with a hotdog in my hand. I stared out over the bay, taking it all in. The sights, the sounds, the dirty smell of the sea and the smoky taste of my junk food.

It was a good night, but it came in on a good tide. The sweet mood was merely an extension, an expression, of what was already true to me; that I was in the right place, that things were going to be fine.

Warm and homely, it also carried an electric note of excitement. It was anticipation, and joy. It washed over me like the lapping sea; it kept on lapping, kept on giving, in waves. It seemed to be almost never ending. I put the whole night on pause, as if to remind myself for a lifetime that such a thing could be true.

I don't know if you've ever felt completely at one with a time and a place, as if you could roll with anything it threw, and be prepared to throw yourself back knowing that nothing would hurt you harder than you could stand? I think it is a better feeling than even believing you will never be hurt at all. It would make such a state seem like sleep.

I concentrated on the feeling, on the horizon, on the glow of the lamps, gold and black, shimmering and distorted in the crests of countless gentle breakers; a satin blanket of a night; warm and glossy, charged and potent.

I don't know how long I stood there. I remember it now as a single experience, suspended like a jewel in the evening, set apart from the minor events, the conversations, the passing of time.

And it occurred to me that I never once felt out of place in St. Andrews. I felt like an idiot plenty of times, like I didn't know what was going on all of the time, and like I was missing out on *something* most of the time. But, if anything, that only made me hungry to see, do, and live a little more. I never felt like I should be anywhere else, not for a moment, not even when I wanted the earth to swallow me.

There were tough times, and melodrama, and I was stupid with my time and with love, and wrong about it, too. But that sponge-like faith in the rightness of it all cushioned every blow. I could shrug off the worst of it, and still feel nothing but harmony and that strange, hopeful, coy expectation.

It was a slight pressure on my shoulder that finally brought me back to the night.

'Are you wearing *trainers*?' a girl in a long green evening dress was asking, with the peculiar nasal shock of the gaspingly rich. She put her hand to her chest, as if to calm herself after a nasty experience.

'Not exactly,' I sighed, wishing the earth would swallow me.

When I found Craig he was chatting to a tall, blonde first-year. I left him to it.

I went to the bar again, where they were now only serving one drink per person. Sandy Bertrando was there, getting outrageously drunk, and pulling out all the stops on his way to oblivion.

'What do you want to drink?' Sandy asked me, a little too showily for a place with a free bar.

'Gin and Tonic,' I said. Sandy frowned, and ordered something else. Something pink.

'Thanks,' I said, as we left the bar.

'Aha! They're both for me,' he said in his typical, mocking whine.

'Of course they are,' I said, with a sigh. I had forgotten what a prick Sandy could be when he was... well. All of the time.

'Yaah! Fuck your system!' Sandy shouted at the barman, downing one drink and running off with the second. His triumphant laughter echoed down the corridor[*].

I couldn't be bothered to join the queue again, so I went off to get another hotdog. I met Craig outside, and we went in together for a last look at things.

'How's your blonde?' I asked.

'She's stuffy and rich,' he said. 'Even her name. Elizabethe. Elizabethe with an extra 'E'. You know why? Because her parents can afford one.'

'You talked for a long time,' I said, reproachfully.

'She's getting a fucking pilot's license. Jesus.'

'I think it's time I tried talking to a girl,' I said, frowning.

'Yeah, well I think It's time to leave,' Craig replied.

'I don't know,' I said. 'I think this could go on all night'.

'Not really,' he said, pointing. 'The police are here.'

---

[*] Bertrando should be hermetically sealed in a vault somewhere in Paris, just to give the world a standard definition for the word 'cackle'.

They stood in the doorway, tearing the drinks out of people's hands, and throwing them to the floor. I wondered how I hadn't noticed them come in.

'The party is over,' one of them shouted into the room. 'Everybody needs to leave, right now.'

We watched them for a couple of minutes, and then snuck out to go home.

Darcy Loch's Whey Pat Flat

I met Darcy in town the next morning, at around two p.m.

'Afternoon, Quinn,' she said.

'Yeahyeahyeah,' I whimpered, unconvinced.

I have no idea what I was in town for, but I remember that I was in pain.

'Fancy a cup of tea?' she asked.

'You had me at tea,' I told her.

'That was the end of the sentence.'

'Fuck.'

'There's biscuits, maybe.'

'You had me at tea,' I said, clutching my head.

Darcy was Craig's ex. Things had gone South, and they had treated each other pretty fucking badly in the death throes of the relationship. Neither of them had much good to say about the other.

'How've you been?' I asked.

'Shitty,' she said. 'Just awful.' She took a deep breath and smiled, with a sharp, bracing exhale.

The previous year had taught me the range of my emotional intelligence, and I knew that I wanted to work up to other people's break-ups.

'I don't know, maybe I should leave you to it?'

'No,' she said, reaching out suddenly. 'Come see my flat.'

She pulled her arm back before it touched mine, but it hovered urgently.

'Where are you staying this year?'

'There,' she pointed.

'In the Whey Pat?'

'Above it. Behind, it, sort of, but round a corner. Come on.'

'Alright,' I said.

We walked down the side of the Whey Pat, past a cute little garden with hanging baskets, and through a little gate, along a wall, around a corner, and back up some stairs to a main door. There was nobody else home.

'There's an old lady in the flat below,' Darcy said. 'You better take your shoes off, because she complains when we walk around.'

'At night?' I said. One of my socks had a hole in it at the big toe.

'No, then it's fine. She sleeps like a log. Just in the day. She's always banging on the floor.'

It was a dinky looking place from the entry way, but there were stairs going upwards. There were clothes drying all the way up the banister. We went into the kitchen, which was also awash with damp laundry, and the hot sickly smell of a freshly run load.

The kitchen overlooked the cute little garden we had passed on the way in. I looked out of the window, while Darcy pottered at the counter. On the opposite side of the road was an old folk's home.

'There's always someone up at night, sitting in that lounge, no matter what time it is,' she said. 'I guess it doesn't matter what time it is when you're old.'

'Old people sleep less,' I said.

'Not less than you.'

'Not less than me.'

'Bourbons okay?' she asked.

I turned back into the room. She was holding a packet of biscuits. I nodded.

'I think I would find it comforting to see them there,' I said, indicating out of the window with my thumb. 'I sometimes just feel like I need to see other people when I can't sleep.'

'You can see me, sometimes,' Darcy said. 'I don't sleep so well, either. Just give me a call.'

'OK,' I said. But I didn't mean it, at least not right then. You can't call someone at five in the morning on the off chance they're still awake.

Darcy put the tea down, and brought over a plate with biscuits on. I had forgotten that Darcy knew me well enough. But she'd been with us, ostensibly one of our group, for most of the first year. She had been Craig's girlfriend, after all. I still felt like she was a stranger.

'I feel like we've hardly talked for ages,' Darcy said. She settled into a high-backed chair on the opposite side of the kitchen table. She cupped her mug with both hands.

'Well, there was the summer,' I said. 'And all the stuff with Craig.'

'He's such a bastard,' she said.

'There's a healthy reflex.'

'Sorry, I know he's your friend,' Darcy said.

'He can be a jerk.'

She sighed, and shrugged.

Darcy wasn't beautiful. Her features were just a bit too round and cherub-like to really be striking and a bit too ordinary to be girl-next-door attractive. But she did have a certain appealing way about her, a certain air that sometimes made her seem like she was really something. At any rate, I could certainly imagine fucking her, so I did that for a while.

'What are you giving me that dopey look for?' Darcy asked.

'Just checking out your eyeliner,' I lied, immediately, while one half of my brain screamed at me that I didn't know what eyeliner was, or if she was wearing any.

'Oh, yah,' she said. 'It's a really nice colour, hmm? It's just from Boots, but I had to go out to Dundee to find one big enough to stock the colours that suit me.'

'They've got like a fucking aisle and a half, in St. Andrews,' I said.

'I know,' she said. 'These tiny *provincial* branches only stock the popular stuff, and that means that people with unconventional colours are out of luck.'

'You have unconventional colours,' I said in a monotone, unsure of the appropriate inflection.

'Yes,' she said. 'And you've got to know your strengths. Take red for example. I can't do red, especially not on the lips. It makes me look like a harlot! I can't do *any* reds.'

'Hmm,' I said. 'You wear *pink* lipstick.'

'You know,' she said. 'You haven't the first idea about any of this.'

'No.'

'Well, what's it like living with him?'

'He's a pain in the arse,' I said.

'I know, right?' she said.

'He's so fucking particular. He demands we put the vegetables into the stir fry in a precise order, or he refuses to eat it.'

'More for the rest of you.'

'Or pay for his share.'

'Oh.'

'And he'll bitch about it all the next day.'

'You liking Fife Park?' Darcy asked. 'I thought it was a shithole.'

'It is,' I said. 'But it's cheap, and...'

'Well,' she said. 'At least it's cheap.'

'No, there's something about it,' I said. 'Something really different. Not like other places I've stayed. It feels like freedom.'

'Well, it's kind of like camping,' Darcy said.

'It's not that bad,' I said. 'Hell, you can live anywhere, if you get on with the people.'

'You know he wanted us to move in together,' she said, suddenly.

'I didn't know,' I said.

'That's why he was dragging his heels over getting the place with you guys.'

'I didn't know. He never said.'

'That boy hates himself,' she told me.

'He hates a lot of things,' I said. 'Let's not start drawing lines.'

'Frank's lovely,' she said. 'He's so nice. You know he's the only person who's said 'Hello' to me since we got back this year.'

'Apart from me.'

'Mart crossed the street to get away from me.'

'Mart just doesn't know what to say,' I said. 'He's not good with awkward situations.'

'It is awkward,' she said. 'I'm so glad you came in for tea. It's not awkward now you're here, right?'

'Well, there's knickers all over the place,' I told her.

'They're not mine,' she said. 'I haven't done laundry yet.'

Somehow that made it easier to look at them.

'Done your Phil essay, yet?'

'No,' she said. 'And neither have you. Even though it's a week late.'

'I've got to worry about Psychology, first,' I told her. 'Fucking stats is my kryptonite. What's your excuse?'

'Better than yours,' she said. 'Saw the dick in English yesterday. Didn't even look my way.'

'That's your excuse?'

'No, fool. I was just saying.'

We sipped our tea, slurping a little at the same time. She laughed. I took another biscuit.

'I remember the first night I knew you guys were in trouble,' I said. 'The James Bond Ball, back at the end of first year?'

'We'd been in trouble for weeks, by then.'

'Yeah, well. That was the first night I knew. You were frosty.'

'Like a Bond villain? I was a bit of an ice queen.'

'Yeah, but you still went through all the boyfriend-girlfriend stuff. Buying each other ice creams and playing games. You weren't into it, though. It was just obvious.'

'Like we were at each other's throats, secretly.'

'No, worse. Like you were desperate to save it and overcompensating.'

Darcy didn't say anything.

'It was just... sad.' I fumbled for words, wishing I hadn't started in on it all. 'You were all over each other, but it was empty. And not like because you didn't mean it. That's why it was sad. Because you really did mean it, but it didn't matter.'

'Well,' she said, eventually. 'I'm sorry our break up was so traumatic for you.'

'No,' I said. 'It was.'

'Well,' she said again, more lightly, 'It's not all roses, all the time.'

I grinned. 'I may never love again.'

'Hey, you had your little crush back then, do you remember?'

That brought the colour to my cheeks.

'Remember?' I said. 'I was wearing a fucking blouse.'

I raised the tea to my lips, and got the cold dregs of the mug. How circular life is.

Thunderballs

The James Bond Ball, a.k.a. Thunderball[*], in First Year was the single worst night I had in St. Andrews. I don't blame the organisers, although it was a bit lacklustre. I don't blame the venue, although the Younger Hall could suck the life out of an orgy with extra tits. No, I blame myself, and I'm glad to have had the opportunity to do so. I should mention that I also slightly blame Craig and McQueen for being such pricks about it all. Later on, I threatened to kill them.

But, if it wasn't for that night, I might never have realised what a precipitous gulf so obviously separated me from adulthood. And I'm not talking about sex or money, here. Those chapters come later and, fortunately, separately. I'm talking about your obvious, usual, common or garden goddamn motherfucking social graces.

At that time I was into a medic called Vikki. She was cute as a button. Button nose. Round cheeks. Wide smile. Really pretty. I really didn't know her at all, but fuck it all, I was still a teenager. I was also an emotionally-stunted idiot.

I had my one big falling out with McQueen over Vikki. It was an old chestnut, thoroughly roasted; McQueen knew that I was into a certain girl, and he wasn't. But when she went for him, he returned the favour. For the fuck of it, I guess, because he unceremoniously dumped her a week later. Just long enough for it to feel insulting both ways.

'The problem is not me,' McQueen said. 'The problem is you. You're the one who made this into something.'

---

[*] Ha fucking ha.

'But you didn't even *care*,' I said.

'And you don't even know her,' he replied. 'So how could you?'

I can't even remember how I followed up on that, but I did. I must have, because it didn't end there by a long way. I didn't listen to Frank. He didn't listen to me. But I don't think we could have understood each other even if we'd been trying.

Of course, for some reason that obviously didn't seem like a double-standard at the time, the logic about Frank not interfering with my potential love interests did not apply the other way around, to myself and his previous ones. I know this because I was still inexplicably determined to make it with Vikki, around the time of the Thunderball. And hell, I reasoned, she was single. Again.

This is what I'm talking about. Who would not just give it up as a bad job by this point? Who would not, for the mere avoidance of awkwardness, drop a stupid and uninvested crush like a hot stone the minute it became inconvenient? All I can offer is that sudden, ridiculous, capricious and unrealistic infatuations are the mark of a young man. If he is also a cunt.

So, the morning of the ball, I went down to the Oxfam on Bell Street, rounding the corner with a spring in my step. Bell Street is possibly my favourite street in St. Andrews. I have no idea why, other than that Aikman's used to be on it. I just always feel a bit brighter on Bell Street. Oxfam on Bell Street was one of my prime haunts for shirts of mass destruction.

I had a thing for shirts that were unorthodox, garish, tasteless, loud, psychedelic, frilly, or whichever combination of the above most narrowly trod the line between 'quietly assured eccentricity' and 'offence punishable by law'. I recognise that this is a character flaw. I'm told that it's the guilty pleasure of many who crave just a bit of attention, but can't offer a compelling reason for anyone to give it. It was a sort of game, and I called it Shirt Attack. That was a stupid name. Orwell would have called it "EyeCrime"[*].

Nice place, St. Andrews. But apart from the students, virtually everyone there is pensionable. You can see why; it might be a lovely place to study or to retire, but St. Andrews holds about as much excitement for your average adult human as a soggy Ryvita. Because of this, the town has a population that consists almost entirely of people who get up at noon, take up interminable residence in coffee shops, and are permanently strapped for cash. Charity shops have flourished[†]. And so did my wardrobe because, frankly, you would be surprised at how much stuff in places like that might set alarm bells ringing in most airports.

Don't get me wrong; I wouldn't just wear any old tasteless thing. It had to be *special.* In second year, I found a shirt that looked like it was made of glitter and mother of pearl, and held together by the silvery excretions of an excitable pixie. That became a staple for a while. My first year favourite had been in

---

[*] That would also have been a stupid name, but at least he would have been able to claim it was satirical.

[†] It's a commonly held misconception that old people love charity shops, but I've never found that to be the case. Old people shop there out of necessity. Virtually everything in a charity shop belonged to somebody who *was* old, and is now dead. Nobody *wants* to shop in that kind of environment. Imagine if Sainsbury's did a 2-for-1 on soap, with the slogan 'maybe you'll be dead before you need any more soap'. That would have to be some seriously cheap soap, on a day you really needed more soap.

orange and blue, and looked like one of Picasso's 'angry period' works. It met a grim fate the night I fell down a nightclub's biggest flight of stairs to what was very nearly my death. I was drunk and arsing about[*]. It was a narrow escape from a fairly typical first-year fatality. The shirt was not so lucky, sustaining a mortal wound that unthreaded it wear by wear until it simply fell apart some time after the start of second year.

Oxfam on Bell Street was also where Vikki did her volunteer shift, which was cynically calculated on my part and, looking back, a bit creepy. I saw her at the checkout on the way in, and almost tripped over my own feet like the suave motherfucker I've always been. I went straight to the shirt racks, and collected myself while browsing through. As usual, a Geiger counter would have been useful. I found some kind of green, blue and violet paint-splashed nightmare of a shirt[†] and, hoping it would be a talking point, I took it up to the checkout.

'You going to the ball tonight?' I asked.

'The James Bond one,' Vikki said. 'Yeah.'

'I think it will be a lot of fun,' I said, in what would turn out to be the least accurate prediction of the day.

'Hope so,' she said, disinterestedly. 'You getting this shirt for tonight?'

'Yeah, I think it will go with my suit,' I said, in what would turn out to be the second least accurate prediction of the day. Vikki didn't even look at it.

'That will be three pounds, please,' she said. I handed it over.

---

[*] My greatest regret is that the scar under my eye has such a worthless back-story.

[†] It was pretty rad. Ba-dum tish.

'Thanks,' I said. Then the conversation was over. I had been looking forwards to it all morning, and it was just a brutal transaction. I walked out of the shop in a daze. The door jangled on the way out, just like it does on the way in.

When I got home, I tried the shirt on. The buttons were all on the wrong side.

'That's because it's a blouse,' Craig said. 'They button up differently.'

'What?'

'Yeah, girls button up everything the wrong way,' McQueen confirmed. 'What you've got there is a blouse.'

'Shit. I can't not wear it.'

'Whatever.'

'No, I told someone I would have it on tonight.'

'That's between you and your blouse,' McQueen said.

'You, your blouse, and a whole bunch of guys, who you will be fucking,' Craig added, 'if you wear a blouse.'

I went back into town, blouse in a carrier bag, wondering whether to ask for my money back. Three pounds. From a fucking charity shop. A student's life is full of such dilemmas.

I sat on the low wall opposite the Union for about twenty minutes, feeling unsatisfied and watching people going in and out of BESS. It's a town small enough I recognised most of the faces. It's a town too small to make the kinds of huge social mistakes I'd already made my share of. I went back to Oxfam, and told Vikki that I was well into her, and wanted to be more than friends.

'Well, I sort of knew that,' she said.

'Yeah.' I said. 'So I'll see you tonight.'

'Probably.'

'Right.'

I didn't mention the shirt. Blouse.

'Shine on you crazy diamond,' Craig said, when I told him. 'That'll make this evening comfortable.'

'It had to be done,' I said, and believed it for a moment. I didn't tell Frank.

The really pathetic thing is that I thought I was brave for making a point of blurting it out like that. When, really, I was just too scared to keep up the act that is courtship for more than a few seconds at a time. The things we realise years too late. One could write a book about it.

I wore the blouse.

Evening rolled around, we got dressed. I had a fucking headache, like storm clouds coming in. It was actually quite a clear night, but the air was muggy.

Scarface and the Dork were security on the door, on a loaner from the Vic. They recognised us as their regulars, and waved us in with nary a look at our tickets. We sat down and started quaffing plastic pints of lager, student-style. There were party poppers and someone filled my pint with pink and blue streamers. I drunk it anyway, with a straw. We passed around a disposable camera and clowned for it.

We walked around a bit, but although there were a lot of little stalls, there wasn't much to do. The air was dead, and there was no one else we knew around. We were all oddly uneasy.

Every conversation stopped before it really started, every drink tasted foul and made us feel worse. Darcy arrived with Vikki late on and Craig dragged her off to dance. He threw her around out there like he was trying to save her from choking. Or induce it. Or both.

I talked to Vikki a bit at our table and it was a normal, boring conversation. I kept wondering when the magic was going to happen[*].

'Hey,' I said eventually. 'Funny story about this shirt.'

Her face soured for a moment, as if the elephant in the room had just pinched one off on the table.

'Yeah,' she said, getting up. 'Excuse me, though.'

She dragged Darcy off to the bathroom, and Craig shot me a look as they passed him. His lips turned up at the edges. He walked over to me.

'Apparently, you're a stalker,' he said.

'No,' I said. 'I just...'

'Yeah,' he said. 'I just heard it from the horse's mouth. So what is *wrong* with you?'

I didn't have an answer. It was fucking stifling in there. I'd been aware of it all night, but it suddenly felt like every breath had a ton of bricks attached.

Frank was smoking outside when I went to get some air. He looked like he was also getting some air. He looked like he wanted it to be different to mine.

---

[*] It wasn't. Obviously.

40

'You followed her into work, and told her you wanted some of it,' he said.

Fucking Craig.

'It's not like that,' I said. 'I told her I *liked* her.'

'Liked her,' he said. 'Like what? She your sister or something?'

'What's that supposed to mean?'

'You like her because you want her,' he said. 'And there's no difference between that and saying it.'

'Well fucking so what? You *didn't* like her and you still fucking...'

'Don't bother,' he said.

'Well.'

'Don't bother. I'm fucking sick of it.'

'*I told you I liked her*,' I said. Whined, actually.

'And? Don't pretend like you were ever going to do anything about it. What, am I supposed to hang around while you put an option on every chick in town?'

'It was only one,' I said.

'This month.' Frank said. 'It was your academic sister last month, yeah?'

'Dude, that is not fair.'

'Do you know what Vikki thinks of you Quinn? Not a fucking thing. She barely knows you. I see her every day.'

'What?' I said, genuinely surprised. 'Left field comment, much?'

'That's...fuck's sake. That's how things happen. I swear you don't know a fucking thing about anything, Quinn.'

41

He turned his head away and spat into the tarmac. Resigned. But I goaded him one last time.

'You're way out of line telling me who I can and can't see,' I told him.

Frank went very quiet. Then, so I could hardly hear, he said:

'Fine, I give up. I fucking give up with you. You can have my fucking cast-offs, Quinn. Just make sure you seal the deal instead of stalking her all over town, because frankly I think it's freaking her out.'

I don't know if it was the words or the tone, but I knew it was fighting talk, where before it had been a kind of tired pity. I knew it, because I didn't have to know a thing about people to know it. That kind of rage is automatic.

'I'll fucking kill you,' I told him. 'I'll fucking kill you!'

I lunged to get a hold of his throat, but he held me at bay like a leaky bin bag. He didn't hit back. He already looked badly over it. But Craig appeared over his shoulder, right on time.

I don't know how long he'd been watching us. I know him, though.

'How could you misunderstand it all so badly?' Craig asked, shaking his head. Lips still curled in an amused smile.

'You too, Craig. I'll fucking do you, too.'

Smile didn't go anywhere. Cruel motherfucker.

The fight was all out of me anyway, but Scarface pulled me off Frank, started waving his finger at me. Doing the bouncer thing. He was surprisingly bad at it for a man with a four inch knife wound across one cheek. Then again, maybe that's why he got stabbed in the face.

'Can't you see I'm fucking done here?' I told him, backing away with my hands raised. Then I shrugged my shoulders like a petulant child and stormed off home.

I sat bolt upright in bed for hours, back at New Hall, trying to come up with a better comeback than 'I'll fucking kill you'. Permutations of the evening running through my head. Apparently I didn't know a fucking thing about anything. How could I misunderstand things so badly? What was *wrong* with me? It was four in the morning when the pictures in my head turned on their side, and I saw it all out of context, with myself as the crazy, irrational, socially-retarded stalker.

Thank God for that moment. An hour later, that was how things were, they'd always been that way, how could anyone not understand that? But it was six in the morning before the right comeback fell into place.

I was wearing my dressing gown when I banged on Frank's door. Took him a while to open it.

'Fucking hell Quinn,' he said.

'I'm sorry,' I said. 'I'm sorry. Can I come in? I need to say some things.'

Frank waved me in, and I sat on a pile of shirts in his chair. But all I said was 'I'm sorry,' again.

'It's fucking 6am,' he said, getting back into bed. 'Why aren't you sleeping it off?'

'I've been up all night,' I said. 'I just feel so bad.'

'You were pretty fucked.'

'I mean, about what I said.'

43

'Don't worry about it, Quinn,' he said.

I could feel the guilt burning in my stomach, and apologising wasn't making it go away.

'Look,' Frank said. 'What I said about Vikki, too.'

'Yeah, it was shitty,' I said. 'But I was so out of line. I just...'

'Forget it,' he said. 'It's done.'

'But, I just feel so *bad*.'

'That's how it is,' he said, with an exasperated sigh. 'Go to bed.'

'Is it OK, though?' I said.

'Fuck's sake,' he told me. 'Go to bed. Get out of here, you big Cunter.'

'...Yeah,' I said.

It wasn't OK. But Frank wouldn't call just *anyone* a Cunter.

Moving and Shaking

So that was me, at my worst. As much of my worst as I can stand to tell, at any rate. Maybe you're thinking that, despite my best efforts, I've come off as a whiny prick. If so, I wouldn't worry about it. The only thing you need to worry about now is that you've made a minor commitment to reading a book about someone who started out as a whiny prick. I feel your pain. Could be that it seems like this is going to be a long read, and for all you know the twist at the end is that I don't have a character arc. I'll do my best to mitigate that.

Let's not forget that you've seen my friends at their worst by now, as well. And, you can trust me, they turned out alright. Frank, who can at times seem cavalier and indifferent is charming exactly because he's so low maintenance, his heart so genuine, his friendship so unshakeable.

And Craig, as particular, fussy, and demanding as he can be… well. I guess the thing about Craig is that he's unshakeable in a different way. Craig is like the Gym teacher who always demands more than you think you have, takes no quarter, has no time for weakness, but leaves you surprising yourself all the same. Although, unlike with the Gym teacher, there is no revelatory moment of acceptance or praise with Craig; you never actually make the grade[*].

I don't hold it against him. He was so consistent and exhaustive in his dissatisfaction, I rather think it might have been its own

---

[*] There's also slightly less inappropriate touching, but not so you'd notice.

punishment. Besides, he was good for me. He was very fucking motivating company, and that shouldn't be underestimated.

Craig pushed me constantly, and I needed it at the time. It doesn't matter that he would have done it anyway, even if I hadn't needed it at the time, or if I only sort of needed it or, hell, if I was just passing. Talk about a moot point. None of it would have been the same without him. I still need him, truth be told. I bet he'd shake me right out of this funk with a few days of belittling and coerced physical exercise.

'It's the gym for you, Butterball,' he'd say. 'Get your bag'.

Later he'd question the quality of my food intake, and then my parentage.

Craig was a peculiarly complementary personality[*], but not a role model. Much as I valued his presence in those formative years, I wouldn't have wanted to emulate him. Frank, though, I don't know. I was jealous of Frank. Frank didn't get fazed, ever, by anything, and I desperately wanted that quality.

Outwardly, Frank had nothing to teach, and he was anything but motivating. He was just a mate, but he always seemed to have the answer. And the answer was always to worry less. Mostly I found it impossible to worry less, but I liked the idea of it. Frank was a reluctant mentor.

'Quinn,' he said, during one tellingly metaphysical chat, 'firstly, the very fact that you're asking for help chilling out worries me so, as you can see, no man is an island. Secondly, if I *were* in a position to offer that advice, it would be – in the nicest possible way – to shut the fuck up and stop listening to the voices in

---

[*] Well, in one sense of the word.

your head, which is also what I'd say if your request made no kind of sense to me, or if I thought you were basically crazy.'

'Thanks,' I said.

'That wasn't advice,' Frank said. 'That was why I'm not giving you any advice. My advice is to roll yourself a man-sized joint, and by yourself I mean us. Gear's on the table – Doctor's orders.'

Divan, Divan

It was freezing cold in my room, because the window was always open if anyone was smoking. We smoked a decent bit of pot in my room, looking back. I never thought of myself as a stoner, but I guess I thought of a lot of my friends that way, and this probably should have clued me in. I wouldn't say I fit the mould, exactly. I guess what set me apart from all the people who just tried it once or twice[*], was that I really kind of liked it. I liked it for what it was, and not for what it represented.

I remember the first time I tried it. Frank introduced me, of course.

'Wanna try a joint?' he asked me, nonchalantly.

'Yeah, okay.' I said.

'Let's go back to my room and skin,' he replied. I had no idea what that meant.

Frank meticulously constructed a joint in his en-suite New Hall bathroom, as I watched wide-eyed. I recall it with the strange duality of the known and unknown. I know how to roll a joint well enough these days, although Frank would still say that I didn't. But I remember the way he made that one joint, before I knew how a joint was made, as a process in abstract. In my memory of the night, all of those steps are still arcane and unfamiliar.

'Now what?' I asked, when he proudly held it up to the light. It looked like a cheap firecracker.

---

[*] Which, by the way, is everyone.

48

'Now we smoke it,' Frank said. Then, seeing that I was still mystified, he added 'like a cigarette.'

'OK.'

'Not in here, though. Smoke alarm.'

We went out for a walk, over the North Haugh, almost to the Old Course, and lit up just off the main road. It was quiet, dark, the stars were bright. My hands were shaking. I thought I could hear dogs barking.

I was always very nervous about smoking hash, which is to say that the thought of getting busted with a spliff sent me spiralling into an almost feral panic. Sure, I didn't see anything particularly *wrong* with smoking it, but the law does not always accord with common sense. I was much more afraid of getting on the wrong side of the law than of getting on the wrong side of common sense, which is something for which I've got an established coping strategy.

I sometimes wonder why I made such an effort to do something that put me so much on edge. I guess that was something of a theme, at the time. But also, it made things seem alright as well. It put me on edge, but it settled me down. It conflicted me, but also relaxed me. Made me calm and terrified. And it somehow seemed to make all the difference at a difficult time, though I suppose it wasn't the smoking so much as the company that mattered.

When I was at my worst that first year, when I stepped right out of line, when I said the wrong things out of spite, or ignorance, or desperation – even when I said those things right to Frank, spat them in his face – he would roll us a joint, we'd take a walk in the night, and we would talk about any other things.

I bought a tiny bit of it towards the end of the year, and kept it like some kind of a prized trophy. I held on to my little block all summer, like a little super-dense piece of the sun, with my tiny world still revolving round it.

When we got back for the second year, Frank was uproariously happy to see that I'd kept a souvenir of the first, because he had run out at the start of the summer, about five minutes before getting into his Dad's car, and being driven home to the East Coast. Apparently it had taken the edge off delivering the news that he'd failed his first preclinical year, but not nearly by enough.

We smoked a joint each day, till the stuff was gone, and didn't even feel the need to go out on a huge hike to find some secluded spot, like we did back in the New Hall days. We smoked right in the room, and even I was happy with that.

Dylan was the first of the Randoms that we really got to know. He caught the smell of it, and came to join us. Dylan was kind of the poster boy for being stoned. He was thin. He was a genius. He was a philosopher mathematician. He was Zen as fuck. He had long, wavy hair, and reportedly looked American[*]. We'd sit together with some of his psychedelic tracks on, and figure we were in the most peaceful place on earth. There was a kind of detached freedom to Fife Park, that gave me peace. The house was a home, not a room. It was ours to enjoy.

I was not *entirely* comfortable, of course. I left the window open day and night, and there was an occasional burst of paranoia, a mild fear of being caught in the act, but nothing like

---

[*] Or like a Cocker Spaniel, depending on who you believe. I think it's the dimple in his chin that does it; the American thing, that is.

I would get when Frank decided to skin up in the toilet of a bar, or casually light up while walking into town. In Fife Park, I felt like I was at home to please myself.

That was until Craig's parents turned up with a cellophane wrapped mattress, and poked their heads around the door while I was skinning up.

'Hi,' I said, my hands wavering over the tray for a moment. We used to roll up on a circular green plastic tray which moved about between Frank's and my room, depending on who'd rolled up last.

'Hi,' Craig's mother waved, unenthusiastically. Her eyes dropped to the tray on my lap.

'Yeah,' I said, in answer to the silence, but the conversation was already over.

They took the mattress next door, dropped off Craig's takeaway, and solemnly left. I mentioned it to Craig later, but he was nonchalant.

'I've already told them that you smoke loads of gear.'

'Betrayed,' McQueen pronounced, authoritatively. 'You are *not* the Eggman.'

Then he picked up Craig's old mattress, dragged it into the hallway, and threw it downstairs.

The mattresses in Fife Park were a joke. They were stuffed with harsh, revolting horsehair[*]. The real irritation, though, was that they were laminated in some kind of waterproof plastic which made it almost impossible to keep a sheet on. Fife Park must

---

[*] We know, because Frank jumped on one, and split it down the side, spewing the coarse, hairy mess onto the floor of my room.

51

have seen a lot of bedwetters the year before, because they'd all been bought to order. The whole Park had these things, brand spanking new, brand spanking awful. You could pour a whole can of Irn Bru onto one of those mattresses, and it would just run off. We know, because we saw it done[*].

The worst thing about them was that they were sticky, clammy, and foul smelling – even through a sheet or two, which would invariably ride up and come off during the night, in any case. No matter what preventative measures you resorted to – doubling the sheets up, taping them down, or covering the bed with an oriental throw – still you were virtually guaranteed to wake up with your face stuck to plastic. We hated those mattresses, but we all made shift with them – all except Craig.

Craig's parents visited him every Tuesday night. They lived in Dundee, only fifteen miles away[†]. They collected his laundry, and invariably brought him some form of takeaway – usually a Chinese. By the second week of the semester, they had also brought him a new mattress, because he didn't like the old one. They brought a standard single mattress, but it hung an unreasonable distance over the side of the bed beneath it, just going to show how small those Fife Park beds were.

McQueen spent at least an hour in the stairwell with the old mattress, proceeding to repeatedly launch himself down the stairs on it with little regard for self-preservation, before clambering back up to the top for another go.

---

[*] Ah, who am I kidding? It was us.
[†] I say 'only'. It turns out that this can be quite a long way, depending on the circumstances.

One time, he veered too far to the right with one of his parasuicidal leaps, and wound up wedged between planks of the thin wooden banister. He gave a couple of high pitched squeals of surprise, and managed to struggle out from his lodgement – but to no avail, because the mattress was too slippery for him to gain any purchase. In the end, he had to pull himself up the length of half the staircase on the banisters alone, all the while laying on his side. He referred to this as a 'superb commando effort' and redoubled his attempts to do himself massive internal injury on the stairwell. I know, because I stood and watched – I was the very picture of vicarious maternal concern.

These hijinks were brought to a sudden end when one misjudged gauntlet run had him slide down the stairs, rather than the mattress, on his belly, before cracking his head into the fire extinguisher at the bottom of the flight. The sound of this went something like *Thump, Thump, Thump, Thump, Ding!*

'Ow,' he reported placidly, and then wandered into the kitchen.

That's one thing worth mentioning about Frank; his tolerance for pain is exceptional. He took a lot worse than that before the end of the year, and never voiced more than a passing concern.

For my part, I tried to avoid pain at all costs. I took the mattress back to my room, and stacked it on top of my own. A double thickness of Fife Park's best probably wasn't as good as a single, ordinary honest-to-goodness mattress intended for people with shoulders and bladder control, but it did mean that I could just pull the spare one out and have an extra bed on the floor of my room, which came in handy on countless occasions*.

---

* Well, it came in handy twice, then Frank jumped on it with both feet, and the resulting explosion covered us in dust and hair, and made my room smell like a stable at mucking out time.

54

The Glow

More and more, as I'm writing, I remember the feeling. I'm talking about that special, particular flavour of the time; that joy, that passion. I don't know what brought it out. I don't know why it went away. I don't know how I let that happen. By inches, probably.

Sometimes, even these days, I catch a trace of it in thoughts. It reminds me of how different my life is, now. If it lingers long enough, and it hardly ever does, it makes me achingly sad. Not just with the touch of bittersweet sadness that is inherent in nostalgia, but a deeper, harder, aimless sadness.

Ella had a perfume. They don't make it any more. I have an empty flask she gave to me.

Sometimes I wave it and breathe deep to catch the last trails of scent. It is still there. It makes me feel hope, and love, and young, and energy – not just energy, but *my* energy. It is so similar to this *glow*, I used to have. There will never be any more of it, and one day soon there will be nothing left to trace in the air.

This glow, I don't even know if I trust it. Embers glow, and it can mean nothing at all.

The Dark Room

It was almost always dark in my room; there were no working lights after the third week of term. This was because Mart, on a visit from DRH[*], had broken the lightbulb. And, more importantly, the fitting. In his defence, he was being an excitable drunk for a change, rather than a miserable one. He was celebrating Frank's failure to break his record, for the fourth time in a row, by dancing with a five foot tall inflatable alien.

When the lightbulb shattered, we were instantly treated to the near ideal combination of darkness and strewn broken glass.

'Oh fuck,' Mart said, miserable again.

'Someone fetch my shoes,' I sighed.

'Shit,' Frank said, from the hotseat at the computer. He brightened almost immediately. 'Guess I'll have to have another go, since I've only got my socks on.'

We were emulating Track and Field, the arcade version from 1983, and my keyboard was taking a pounding from all the button mashing. Frank didn't *only* have his socks on – he was also wearing a pair of red and blue plaid boxer shorts, and an old grey T-shirt.

'Fuck you,' Lance said, pulling from his Stella. 'It's been my go for about an hour.'

---

[*] David Russell Hall was also a shithole, but most residents believed it had the best community spirit in St. Andrews. People certainly do seem to band together in adversity.

Frank kept playing. Lance didn't care, as long as nobody took his Stella away.

'Dude,' Mart said. 'I don't think you should drink that. It might have broken glass in it.'

Even in the glow from the monitor, you could see Lance's knuckles whiten against the side of his pub-style pint glass[*].

'You... *fuckers*,' he said.

'Get the dustpan from the kitchen, would you Mart?' Frank said, dismissively.

'And grab a stubby for Lance,' I added. 'There's still a few in the fridge.'

'And one for me,' Frank chanced.

'Come on, let's go out,' Lance growled, impatiently. 'Get some jars in.'

'If I get you the kit, can you just hook him up to one of those stubbys?' I asked Frank.

'We haven't covered intravenous stuff, yet,' Frank said, cautiously.

'Can't hurt to be ahead of the curve this year,' I said, meaningfully.

'We're going out,' Craig announced, tugging at his shirt cuffs as he entered the room.

'Finally,' Lance said.

'Watch it, Craig,' I said. 'There's broken glass everywhere.'

'Then why are the fucking lights off?'

---

[*] All of our pint glasses were 'pub-style', because they were all stolen from pubs.

57

'That's what's broken,' Lance said. 'It went in my beer.'

'Now it's a light beer,' Frank told him. 'Drink up. Bit of broken glass never hurt anyone.'

Lance looked down at the beer. It was touch and go. I reached over and took the pint away from him; the glass came free from his hand on the third try.

'Shouldn't you be the responsible one?' I asked Frank, a bit harshly. He looked at me, quizzically.

'Why?' he said, like I'd just asked if he wanted to fuck a Husky.

'Because you're a fucking doctor,' I said. 'Or you will be.'

'Might be,' Craig interjected.

'...might be a doctor,' I finished, corrected. 'People are going to take you seriously!'

'We can't all be philosophers, Quinn.'

Mart walked in with an armful of stubby bottles, and passed them around. Lance was not placated.

'Are we fucking going out?' Lance asked. 'Or are we going to sit here chinwagging all night, with beers in our hands?'

I sighed. I don't know the significance of out. I don't know as there's ever been a night I'd have rather gone out with friends than stay in with them. The beer's cheaper, the seats are comfier, the video games don't cost a quid a go. But I've always been boring like that.

'What exactly do you think is going to be different about the Vic tonight?' I asked. 'Because what we do there, we're doing here, only without some cunty drunk caddy spitting in your ear and pishing down his leg.'

That incident was still fresh and it was going to stick with us.

'There's other reasons to be out,' Lance said, genuinely affronted. 'Puppies!'

I looked to Mart. It sounded like a London thing, he was close enough.

'Boobs,' he explained. 'Lance wants to *make it with the ladies*.'

'Lance is going to sit and drink beer and smoke fags,' Craig said.

'And it wouldn't be much of a reason to go out anyway, since none of us ever score.'

'Ella's going out apparently,' Craig told me. 'Heard it from Kate.'

'That's different,' I said, getting up and calmly walking out of the room.

'He's getting his coat,' Frank called after me.

'I'm taking a piss,' I shouted back, guiltily.

I locked the bathroom door behind me and looked into the mirror. It would have to do. Shaving wasn't an option, given the state of my razor. Not unless I wanted to look like a meth addict.

Not for Ella. Ella was special. Ella was beautiful, she was talkative – very talkative, as it happens. There were no awkward pauses with Ella, which had led me to feel almost comfortable talking with her. She had long straight auburn hair, pale skin, and an attractive and consistent smile. She had a beautiful voice. Fortunately.

Coincidentally, she also happened to have lots of other more than appealing qualities which I didn't notice at the time because, on the face of it, Ella was another irrational crush.

'They all start that way,' I said to myself, rationalising. 'It's what you make of it that counts.'

I was making a hash of it. But it was going better than any other attempt so far. At that time of course, I had no idea that it was going to be such a significant crush, or how significant my walk of shame would eventually be. Back then, I just was hoping things would go well. Not that I expected them to, but I was damn well keeping my sheets clean.

'I think there's glass in your bed,' Mart called through the door.

'Thanks, Mart,' I called back. 'I'll be sure to remember that when I get in half-cut at three in the morning.'

'Yeah, you want to hurry up in there?' Mart said. 'I've got business to take care of.'

Mart has legendary bowels.

'Downstairs, you stinky fucker,' Frank shouted from his room. Mart ignored him, and bombed into the john as I left. Craig was pacing in the hallway. He was impatient – not because he was in a hurry for anything in particular, but because waiting for people burns Craig like holy water.

'Where's Frank?' Craig asked.

'Changing his shirt,' I said.

'Change yours?' he asked. I shook my head.

'It's my lucky shirt,' I lied. It wasn't, of course. I'm not sure if I had a lucky shirt. Probably just all the ones I nearly died in, but didn't.

'No blouse tonight?' Frank asked, emerging in a laid back stripy number.

'I lent it to Paedo,' I said.

'You hear he's going out with Vikki, now?'

'Yeah,' I said. 'He may not realise it's a blouse.'

'Come ooooonnnn,' Lance said, waving his empty stubby in the doorway. It was time to go out.

'Mart's in the can,' Craig said.

Unbidden, we went downstairs and waited for Mart outside. In the rain.

Ella wasn't in the Vic, and neither was Kate. The Vic had just exactly everyone who was always in the Vic, including all of us. There were locals fighting over the pool table, and drunk mutton wandering around them in miniskirts looking for a nasty lay. We sat drinking beers, not playing track and field. Lance was happy.

'Alright,' I said, to total indifference. 'Let's go to the union after this one.'

'What's so different about the union?' Lance asked. 'We're just going to sit around and drink beers there, only they'll be worse beers.'

'Damn your logic,' I said. To be fair, the union was the only place on earth that Lance wouldn't settle for the house lager. Union Carlsberg was 1.45 a pint, and smelled like eggy farts and chip fat.

'Yeah, I'm happy here,' Mart said. This was a lie. Mart was never happy after five pints. In another pint he'd start talking about how shit St. Andrews was, and two further down the line it would all get political. It wouldn't be Saturday if he didn't call *someone* a fascist.

'This man wants a bit of Ella,' Craig said, eventually.

I nodded, at last. Grateful not to be the one bringing it up.

'Come on guys,' I said. 'She's bound to be there, and I'm really pulling out the stops this time.'

'He's hardly been annoying about it at all,' Craig said, in admirable defence.

'Sounds like this could be the one,' Frank said, chuckling.

'Schlong says you should just get in there and pull her,' Lance said. He did a hand motion, that was not an analogue to pulling someone.

'Yeah, I'm going to go ahead and file that under controversial advice to be followed as a last resort.'

'Fine, we'll go to the union, just for Quinn,' Mart said.

'No pressure,' Frank told me.

'Can we at least wait until it's busy, though?' Mart asked.

'Reasonable request,' I said. 'What's on tonight, anyway?'

As usual, this was a stupid question to ask in St. Andrews[*].

'I think they're having a Cheesy night at the Bop,' Craig said, without much enthusiasm.

'Great,' Mart sighed. 'How will we tell?'

The Bop, like most events, was in decline in our second year. In the first year, people had made an effort with the events. There had been bands and comedians that we had heard of, and they had even hosted foam parties[†] some nights. It was an euphoric

---

[*] By the third year, we would often ask 'What's on... in Dundee?'
[†] Mart had cracked his chin open while sliding around one night, and then there were no more foam parties.

but short lived phase of our lives although, to be honest, the foam parties were pretty rank. At the height of the foaming we were looking at about a half an inch coverage of wet suds, which dissolved into a slippery mess less than thirty seconds after they turned off the foam sprayers. Luckily, we weren't measuring fun by volume of foam.

The important thing about those days wasn't that they were particularly good; it was that people were willing to throw themselves around in filthy wet shite until injuries took them out of the game. By our second year, everything was just a little bit more reserved, and everyone had just a little bit less enthusiasm. The Bop itself had devolved into three hours of bad music with three people dancing to it. We went every week.

'Guys, are we really going to do the *Bop* again?'

'What else?'

'Fuck's sake,' Mart said. 'St. Andrews is just so fucking *lame*.'

Craig caught my eye.

'The eight-fifteen from Downersville is a little early into the station tonight,' I said, nodding at Mart.

'We should get him over to the union before he starts challenging authority,' Craig agreed.

We got into the Union without too much trouble. Mart got IDed, and refused to show his student card until the bouncer had let Mart identify *him*. Fortunately the guy on the door was new, and thought this was a gag.

'You're going to have fun, here,' Craig told him, as he let us pass.

'We're just a bunch of loveable jokers,' I said, giving him a thumbs up.

'You know what's a joke?' Mart asked. Craig hurried him through the door before he could finish. 'The fucking service around here,' Mart said triumphantly, to the foyer. I glanced back at the doorman, but he was onto the next bunch of customers.

'Jesus,' Craig said. 'He's all yours, I'm going for a slash.'

The queue for the Bop was all around the main doors, and folded back on itself till it was almost into the main bar. It's always fucking all or nothing.

'Better get in the queue,' I said.

I saw Ella towards the front of the queue, and waved. She waved back.

'I'm going to ask her out,' I said to Mart.

'Go for it,' he said.

'Everybody knows you're into her,' Lance said. 'All her friends, too.'

'Ah, good,' I said. No chance for a quiet, private moment of failure then. I took a deep breath. The queue was good for another half hour at least. Plenty of time to steel myself.

I think I asked Ella out three or four times, in second year. I don't know, it didn't seem nearly as pathetic and drippy in person. There was always a good reason to have another shot, or at least it seemed like that. Anyway, I'm a firm believer that we should measure ourselves by our progress and, as such, I consider my numerous and abject failures with Ella as amounting to a kind of success.

For example, I certainly didn't follow her around like a drooling puppy, and I credit myself with having reached a stage of emotional development where this was an obvious decision. I was also able to conduct a conversation of any required length with Ella.

This was more down to her than to me. Ella was always happy to chat, even if I did sometimes make a fool of myself. It was a while before we got to be really *good* friends, I guess this kind of stuff has to be behind you before that can happen. But we were friends. It was nice.

I only remember the first and the last time she turned me down. This was the first. I walked over to her and said a few things, and she cut me down in seconds. I expected to feel horrible about it, but actually it really didn't seem so bad.

'I'm not really at that place in my life,' she said.

It was a good answer, but it was not an answer to the question I had just asked. I had asked her if she knew what our friends were saying about us. Which was lame, I guess. But I wasn't expecting a stock reply quite so soon. It was over already.

'OK,' I said. 'Sure, OK.'

It kind of was OK, as well. We were still chatting, I hadn't threatened to kill anyone yet, and I wasn't even close to being labelled a sex pest. Then she offered me a really awful roll-up that she'd tried to make. It smoked pretty good, considering. I don't know what we talked about after that, but it didn't seem like the worst conversation I'd ever had. When I finished the smoke, I stood up.

'See you later,' I said. She smiled. I smiled back, completely despite myself.

'How'd it go?' Mart asked, when I got back.

'She's washing her hair,' I said. 'For the foreseeable future.'

'Really?' he asked.

'No,' I said. 'But she might as well be.'

'Bummer,' Frank said.

'I guess. She likes me, though. Not like *that*, but as someone to talk to. I can tell.'

'I hate to break it to you mate,' said Mart, 'but I'm pretty sure that goes for everyone. She's a real talker.'

'OK,' I said. 'So I'm as good as everyone else at talking. That's a fucking start.'

'You're not as good as her,' Frank said. 'I ran into her in Woollies the other day, and I couldn't get away.'

'Tell me about it,' Lance said. 'I tried to bum a fag off her last week. Should have just gone to Off Sales.'

'Gonnae give up while you're ahead this time, Quinn?' Frank said, a note of worry in his voice.

'Yeah,' I said, meaning it. That was when it felt worst, right there. 'Let's talk about something else. Where's Craig?'

'Being more successful than you,' Frank said. He pointed.

Craig stood a few feet away, beer in hand, chatting to Elizabethe, the girl he met in Freshers Week.

'I think he's in there,' Lance said. He made another hand sign. It was a pretty good analogue for being 'in there'.

'He's been standing there like that since we got our bop bands,' Frank said.

As it happens, Craig stayed right there until closing time, stuck in the same spot, barely even shifting his weight, like some immoveable pillar at the centre of the Beer Bar. Elizabethe was *not* a talker. Craig was not a talker, either. It was not a conversation. It was a battle of wills that would rage for an eternity. Craig gets drawn into things, and will not let them go. He didn't like her much, or so he always said, but he wound up seeing her on and off for the next four years. If it had been any kind of relationship it would have been the most enduring one of his life.

'I don't know how he does it. Why can't I just strike it lucky, Frank?' I said.

'Dunno,' he said. 'But you're doing it wrong. Asking a girl out shouldn't feel like sitting a driving test.'

'Still doing it wrong,' I said. 'Fuck.'

'I let them come to me,' Frank offered. 'That way I know they're bothered.'

'Shit, Frank,' I said. 'I've been waiting two decades, I figured it couldn't hurt to make some kind of an effort.'

'Yeah, but you were wrong though,' he said. 'Hurts like a bitch.'

'And, what? I should stop caring? That's what you've got? That's bullshit.'

He looked at Craig.

'Well, you could try being more of a cunt.'

We didn't speak to Craig for the rest of the night, and he disappeared with Elizabethe during the last song. Later we found out that he'd invited her out for dinner, and he summarily took her, just a few days later. He took her to the Vine Leaf, hoping to impress her. He was to be sorely disappointed.

He came home at five in the morning complaining that she'd cost him a bona fide fuckton to wine and dine and hadn't, so far as he could tell, actually fucking noticed. Apparently she was horrendously snobby, and her parents had a house the size of New Hall. Then he announced that he had experienced a 'most random night', more to make us jealous than anything else, and went to bed 'shagged out'. I didn't feel all that jealous. Frank didn't even look up from the game he was playing on my computer.

I don't know why we were up at five am when he came back; I think that perhaps we just usually were.

Theme Park

The Fife Park year was all change. Maybe change is the theme of this book. But if that's true, then it's a cop out, because change is the theme of life, and the theme of fiction, and the theme of causality, and the theme of reason and the theme of love and growth and time and friendship and joy and work and everything else that is not the same as it was, which is pretty much everything.

If I could pick a theme for my own book, it would be this mysterious *glow* I'm looking for. It would be that happy, joyful, electric excitement that I felt running through everything back then. It would be that eagerness, that willing, that enthusiasm. But that would imply a level of control that I don't have. Does anybody really choose their own theme? I hardly even think we choose our lives, let alone the narrative.

Back then, I found a project for change, and for years I credited it with success. It was a pop-psychology solution pieced together from cereal packets and lecture notes, and I thought I had it all figured out. If I'd written this book aged twenty-five, it would have been central to the story: how a man can change. Fuck me, I might have even called it that[*].

But I was carried away with the illusion of control. Now I'm more sceptical. Change is a wild, untamcable thing. There is romance in the idea that people change out of will, that they can be made whole again by effort. But I don't believe it.

---

[*] *How a Man Can Change*, that is, not *Fuck Me*. I might yet write that one.

Sure, you can make a change. You can always make a change. You can't look for something and find nothing in this life, it is too full. But it is just any change, desultory and undirected. Serendipity is the Queen of change; you almost never get what you are looking for.

Maybe you sense the paradox in this book. Why am I looking for what I used to be, if I don't believe I chose it even then? What is the point of looking for what can't be found? When finding it would be no guarantee of understanding it. When understanding it would bring me no closer to reviving it. Why trace over old footsteps, if the path will always be a lost one?

Well, maybe finding anything is better than not looking. Or perhaps looking for something is that specific thing I am looking for. Who doesn't love a paradox? Maybe that fluidity, that flexibility, is its own release. And, I suppose I just wonder, if I am *looking* for serendipity, what will I find?

Darcy Loch's Pub Golf Hole-in-one

Fuck me, but Darcy Loch could drink.

Still does, but we don't feel the same about it now. When you're nineteen, it's a badge of honour at worst. The people with the problems and the people without are indistinguishable to a nineteen year-old.

She's a city girl these days; fits right in, holds down some high-powered job, makes things happen, hires and fires and wins awards, takes the pressure. Drinks it all in, like it was a chilled Sancerre. I don't know her any more, but I still know her. We go way back.

The first time we got wrecked together was sometime right before Raisin Weekend. It was a dark night, late autumn, kitchen of her flat. I was still crushing hard on Ella. Darcy was still bitching on about Craig half the time. I got snobby with a bottle of nasty chardonnay and refused to let it sit in the glass[*].

'Fucking awful,' I gagged. 'I'll be glad when we've finished it.'

'You are *such* a woman, Quinn,' Darcy said.

She filled my glass, and topped up her own, with all the wobbly determination of the drinker. She poured until the bottle was vertical. There was nearly enough room in the glass.

'Woah, woah,' I called, as it began to overflow.

A brim of golden-green liquid hung on the rim of the glass like olive oil before breaking ranks and flowing thickly over the

---

[*] The best white wines are Chardonnays. And so, overwhelmingly, are the worst. 'Three for a tenner' deals put you at the gag-reflex end of the spectrum.

edge. Darcy ran her finger up the side of her glass, catching the greasy rivulets until they overflowed onto her pink painted nails.

'Down it,' she said, raising the glass to her lips, shakily. 'And quit bitching.'

I did, getting chunks of dry cork in my throat. I choked. Wine went down the front of my shirt, which fortunately did not look out of place.

'You total arse,' Darcy said, slamming my back.

'Well, the red will be better,' I told her between breaths.

'Want to see if we can drink that one faster?' she asked.

'No.'

'*Woman.*'

'Nothing like a bit of peer pressure,' I said.

'It's got to be all gone less than thirty seconds from pulling the cork,' she told me, screwing in the opener.

'Why?'

'Because it'll put hairs on your chest,' she said. 'I swear, you wouldn't last five minutes in Ireland.'

'I'm so glad I spent all that time picking it out.'

'You are such...'

'Just fucking open it,' I said. I got bigger glasses from the cupboard.

'They're not mine,' she said.

'We can wash them.'

'Thirty seconds,' she reminded me.

Pop. It took thirty-eight.

'Shit,' I said, sitting back. 'We're going to feel that.'

Even she looked like she thought it would be enough.

'How are you doing?' she asked, eventually.

'We drank a bottle of wine in half a minute.'

'Generally, I mean. We haven't talked for days.'

'Huh, really?'

'Yes, really,' she said, sourly. 'Glad you noticed.'

'I've been busy.'

'Liar.'

'I'm into this girl, Ella.'

'Tell me about her,' she said.

I did.

'She sounds nice,' Darcy told me.

'Think she's in the Vic tonight,' I said. 'With all the guys.'

'That bastard there, too?'

'Yeah,' I said. 'All of them.'

'You're missing out?'

'See how much I care?'

'Enough to drink wine with me, instead of beer with the girl of your dreams?'

'That much. Exactly right, except I would be drinking Gin and Tonic.'

'Aww,' she said. 'I'll buy you a Gin and Tonic some time.'

'To be honest, I asked her out and she said no. Ella, I mean.'

'When?'

'Last week maybe? The week before? I don't know.'

'But you're still into her?'

'She's nice,' I said. 'Like I described her.'

'Not that nice, if she turned you down.'

'I've turned people down before,' I said. 'She was nice about it.'

She punched my shoulder.

'You fucking pushover.'

'You don't know her,' I said.

'Still think you're in with a chance?'

'Who knows.'

'You seem different,' she told me. 'Have you lost weight?'

'Doubt it,' I said. 'I've got this plan, though.'

'To lose weight? You don't need to.'

'To seem different. No, I mean, to *be* different.'

'Huh,' she said. 'Oo-kay.'

'Telling,' I replied.

'No, it's not that,' she said. 'You don't need to change.'

I looked at her. She looked at her feet.

'My decision, anyway,' I said.

'Go on. Tell me about your plan, then.'

'Yeah.' I cleared my throat. 'Well, basically you can choose how you behave, but not how you feel, right?'

'Sometimes you can choose how you feel.'

'Yeah, but basically, you like some things, you don't like others, you're good at some things, bad at others, and so on.'

'Whatever.'

'Well, I think that if you pretend to feel a certain way for long enough, it can start to be how you actually feel, not just what you pretend.'

'So if you feel sad, but you pretend to feel happy, then you'll feel happy eventually?'

'No, it's more like... Well, OK, maybe. That's an OK example I guess.'

'Yeah, I don't think so. I think that if you bottle things up and pretend they're different, it can make you sick inside.'

'Well, something else then. Little things. Just like, your body language can tell your mind how to feel, almost as much as the other way round, so you just *act* like something, and it can happen. If you pretend not to be nervous, sometimes it will go away. Or if you pretend to like beer for long enough, you might actually start to like it.'

'What if you feel tired?'

'I don't know, maybe you can ignore it. You might get a second wind, or something. I don't think it's the same sort of thing.'

'But eventually you'll fall asleep or die, or whatever.'

'What I'm saying is that some things, like the way you react to things, might just be something you can train yourself to react differently. So if you're always panicking, you can just pretend to be calm, and it might work.'

'Except, if you're panicking, you won't remember to do anything you decided to do. That's what panic is.'

'Well, I'm talking about if you're just not confident. You could just pretend to be confident. You could just act all laid-back, and not caring, and relaxed, and maybe eventually you'll just feel that way. It sounds calm, and like a pretty cool way to live.'

'Wow,' Darcy said, bored. I'm not sure that I was finished, but she obviously was.

'Yeah, well. That's the plan.'

'You know it makes no sense,' she said. 'Not really.'

'I've been told as much,' I said. 'And you sounded just like him.'

'Fuck off.'

'I think it's a great plan,' I said. 'It all fits together.'

'Are you just pretending to be Frank?' Darcy asked.

'No,' I lied. 'But there's more to it, anyway.'

'Why?'

''Cause Frank doesn't want anything, and I do.'

'Well, I just think you just need to grow up,' she told me, sadly.

'Sorry?'

'I don't mean that in a harsh way. I just think you need to grow up, and it will happen by itself.'

'Well, that's good you don't mean it in a harsh way,' I said. 'Because it sounded like a bitch-slap.'

'You know, I think of girlfriends my age as women,' she said, abstractly. 'But all the boys are still boys.'

'That's sexist as fuck,' I said.

'It's just what I think. Boys mature later.'

'Not always.'

'Well, do you feel like a man?' she said.

'It's not for you to say.'

'That's why I'm asking you.'

'It's not for me to say, either.'

'Oh, convenient. So who?'

'Well, when it's true it's just obvious. Nobody has to make a fucking decision on it.'

'Well, there's your answer.'

There was a tang of sulk in the air that probably didn't help my case.

'Fine, but that doesn't automatically make you a woman.'

'Oh come *on*, Quinn,' she said, leaning over and slurring.

I turned away.

'Alright, look,' she said, conciliatorily. 'Let's go out there and get you some Gin and Tonic.'

'Right now? Seriously?'

'Yeah, it'll be fucking hilarious. We'll just pretend it's an ordinary night out, and go get some drinks in down at the Vic,' she said. 'Just imagine what they'll think when we waltz in there together, like nothing happened.'

'Yeah, it's the wine talking,' I said.

'Doesn't make it a bad idea.'

'What about Craig?'

'Meh,' she said.

'But you're sure you won't regret it?'

'Blah, blah, blah.'

She made a 'chatty' hand motion.

'Whatever. I'll get my coat.'

We sauntered into the Vic like we had a point to prove. Darcy was dead right about the reaction, I wouldn't have credited it. Mouths dropped open. Pints hovered between face and table. Lance's fag went out in the ashtray. Eventually the silence started to seem kind of rude. Mart stepped up to insulate the awkward.

'Fucking hell, Darcy,' he said. 'How in the hell are you?'

'You know,' she said. 'Getting on.'

'Alright Craig,' I said.

'Quinn.'

'Frank not out?'

'Medics,' Craig said. 'Frank's doing all the first year socials again.'

'And the second year ones,' Lance said.

'What have you been up to?' I asked.

'Beers,' Lance said. He raised his pint, grinning.

'Look,' I started.

'This is not cool, Quinn,' Craig said. 'Not cool at all.'

I looked round. Darcy was at the bar.

'Yeah,' I said. 'It's nothing, don't get riled.'

'What are you fucking doing with her?' he asked.

'She's alright,' I said. 'Just some drinks.'

'She's a waste of fucking space.'

'Too harsh, mate.'

'Easy,' said Lance. 'She's right there.'

'You're being a dick,' Craig said.

'We're all of her friends right here.'

'Whose fucking fault is that?'

'I don't fucking know. Not all hers.'

'What about her other friends? Julia?'

'Who fucking knows what happened there?'

Those two had switched poles right at the end of the year, and gone from inseparable to repulsed by each other, over fuck only knows what personal bullshit.

'Mate, she's just not worth it,' Craig said.

'It's not an effort,' I said. 'I'm going to help her with the drinks.'

Darcy was counting small change out of a huge purse at the bar.

'Is it weird?'

'How would I know?' I said.

'Does it seem weird?'

'Fuck, yes.'

'Should we leave? Should I just go?'

'No, I think people are adjusting.'

'It's like they don't even know me.'

'They're on edge,' I said. 'They don't know what to say.'

'Is Ella out?'

'Yeah,' I said. 'At the far table, with the DRH lot.'

'Let's go over,' she said.

'I don't know.'

'Fucking, shut up. I'm not going to embarrass you. But you have to introduce me.'

'Introduce you?'

'Yes, and do it properly.'

'Alright,' I said. 'I hope you're in the mood for a proper conversation.'

She didn't get that, but it didn't take long.

'Hey Quinn,' Ella said.

'Ella,' I said. 'This is Darcy. She's a friend of mine. She wanted to meet you.'

'Oh, nice. Hi Darcy. Why do you want to meet me?' Ella said.

'She wants to meet all my friends,' I said. 'Because she is completely wasted.'

'Quinn!' Darcy said.

'It's OK,' I said. 'It's OK. We're all wasted here.'

'Well, I'm alright,' Ella said.

'Fuck. Of course you are. Why wouldn't you be?'

'Quinn,' Darcy said, pulling me to one side.

'Darcy, this is a *terrible* idea. I think she's fucking sober.'

'You are a fucking moron, Quinn,' Darcy said. 'I'll fix this, you just keep your mouth shut.'

'Yeah, OK.'

'Ella,' Darcy said, with a flourish. 'Aren't you in our Philosophy class – *The Good Life*?'

'Yeah,' Ella said. 'I just put in the essay today.'

'Us too,' Darcy said. 'This fool helped me after my PC ate the file. It's fucking handy having a geek around. '

'Hey,' I said.

'Oh, shut up,' Darcy said. She turned back to Ella. 'He *so* is.'

'And it is a thankless fucking task,' I muttered.

'What did you write about?'' Ella asked.

'Eudaimonia,' Darcy said. 'It's a looooad of bollocks.'

'Change,' I said. 'Question 3.'

'Yeah,' Ella said. 'Me too. Change, I mean. I wrote about how most people want things to be different but hate it when things change.'

'I reckon most people want things that don't make sense,' I said, meaningfully.

'And then philosophers put them into words,' Ella said, clapping her hands together.

I walked Darcy home that night, arm around her shoulder. We went the long way, which is to say that we went the short way, with a lot of zigzagging. Darcy was unusually quiet as we came up on the Whey Pat. She rubbed her eyes.

I was half scared she might pass out completely, leave me dragging her like so much dead weight down City Road. She used to do that, clock off like a light going out, be properly unconscious for hours. We used to think it was something that just happened to her, but I think it's something that happens to anyone, eventually.

'They won't be my friends,' she wailed, suddenly.

'They still like you,' I said. 'Mind the steps.'

'It's not the same,' she said, stumbling.

'Mart was really genuine.'

'It's never going to be the same.'

'You never know,' I said.

She looked at me, appreciatively. But also like I was an idiot.

'You're like my Dad, sometimes,' she said. 'He's such a smart man. He does whatever he wants.'

'I don't do what I want,' I said.

'He just tells people how it's going to be, and then they do as he says. He was always telling us stories about his work.'

'He sounds nice,' I said.

A chill wind hit, as she stood at the top of the stairs to her flat. I stood at the bottom, looking up. She shivered for a second, and then smiled again.

'Ella's so lovely.'

'So lovely,' I said.

She pushed the key into the door on the third try, and stepped inside.

'See you,' I said.

'Night, hun.'

Media Sift

I found some old chat logs in a lost folder of my Fife Park archive. You never really remember anything, right. I spent hours poring through my youthful conversations looking for gold, but it was all mundane and teenage.

I found my old Final Fantasy 8 save games; that's where February went, in the Fife Park year. I'd forgotten that. I found a box of photographs. I looked happy, of course. Sometimes I was thinner than I remember ever being.

I used to skip meals, for days on end. I remember it as a montage, some Rocky-style weight loss video, all fast cuts and motivating music. But, now I think about it, I kind of tortured myself. For months, for nothing, because I didn't realise that my weight had fuck all to do with how likely I was to get laid, to meet someone, to be popular.

I found old emails from Darcy. And emails to Darcy. She would send me a page of nothing at all, and I'd try to be precocious when I replied. It's nothing like I remember. Every time I think of myself, I look differently.

I've still got the music, too. I keep that folder of pirate MP3s safe as houses, backed up across a multitude of sites, because it is the most direct line I have to these memories.

These memories put me in the mood for more than just memories. I'm remembering things, but also feelings, and some old feelings can be bought for a price. I put out the word that I wanted some cannabis.

It has been years since I bought dope. I've hardly even touched it since St. Andrews. Took about two fucking weeks to get some, so nothing new there. I don't know any drug dealers, or have any friends with pretensions to know any. But somebody sorted me out.

I didn't specify the type. I went through a friend of a friend who didn't even know there were types. So, when it came, it was a little mystery gift. I almost forgot I'd asked for it. I kind of hoped it would be hash, but of course it was skunk. What else is there?

I made a single joint and smoked half of it before putting it out. Later I smoked the rest. McQueen would have called me a lightweight. I can hear his voice in my head, just imagining it. But I have always been cautious, and one of the main reasons is because, just occasionally, I haven't been cautious enough. I wanted to be pretty stoned, of course. I wanted to remember that feeling, and all the little things that go along with it.

It was still the same.

The much and too much of it; the shivering, hysterical diaphragm, all giddy butterflies and nerves; the discretion of noise – those noises! The willingness and ability of the ears and the mind to put some hundreds of echoes of small sounds back into the mix, the drops and tinkles and audio also-rans that the senses would otherwise completely discard, but which cannabis makes sound so rich, and seem so planned.

I have had this feeling a lot of times.

It is its own thing. It sinks me into a very unique contentedness. But it wasn't the feeling I was looking for. It's not the answer to the question that is this book. The happy pleasantness of cannabis is just a holiday from whatever you're feeling right when you smoke it. If I'm honest, that's why I smoked it in the first place. Even in Fife Park, there were times it made sense to take a break from everything else. Heck, maybe especially in Fife Park. It was a learning curve, for all its well-aged warmth.

I threw on some music, feeling like a tourist in my own stories. Tried to think what would sound best, what would bring it back most. That's when I remembered what I'd been listening to, on the night I left a note for myself, jotted down on a square of blue paper, and wedged under the feet of my Hi Fi.

I put on *Media Sift...* and closed my eyes.

Green Themes

We made a lot of stir fries in Fife Park, which is to say that Craig and I made a lot of stir fries. We made one almost every night for the first few months. Craig was especially particular about how to prepare his stir fries, and we laboured together each day to meet those exacting standards.

Cooking a stir fry in Fife Park was an exercise in patience. On their maximum settings the hob rings turned a kind of mild orange in colour and heated things more or less to the point they'd eventually dry out, if not cook in any conventional sense of the word. We'd spend an hour or more of our day devoted to the preparation of such a meal, with a good sauce, making it all from scratch out of basic ingredients. They were healthy, substantial meals and damn tasty, but the main point in their favour was that they were not pasta. After the first year, pasta needed to spend a while off menu.

I was glad of the stir fries because, despite Craig's insistence on perfection, it was good to get something healthy inside me. Frank, for example, did not eat stir fries. Frank used to eat Tomato Soup and toast. Sometimes he would eat nothing else for days. Occasionally he'd splash out and pour a can of baked beans over a four pack of sausage rolls.

But for the Grace of God, I say; if it weren't for Craig, I doubt I would have fared even so well as that. I am an atrocious animal. Left to my own devices, I would probably have eaten Frank's leftovers with a tin of Tesco Value peach slices[*].

---

[*] ...which were down to nine pence a tin during the price wars of '99/2000.

I eat bad things. I eat wrongful things, in the name of hunger and of discovery. I will eat things that are barely even food, things that don't look like normal food, things of unknown provenance and uncertain status, things, in short, that normal people would probably not want to touch with their bare hands.

That's how, one mild autumnal night, after eating a stir fry and a semicircle of cremated pizza, I got more stoned than ever before. It was a very interesting experience. It wasn't entirely pleasant, and I was glad when it was over. Afterwards, I wanted to do it again.

On the night in question, Frank had decided to crumble half a nub of resin and use it to season his thin-and-crispy margarita. Inside of a few minutes, the kitchen smelled of gear. In fact the whole house and a good proportion of Fife Park smelled of gear. It was a wholesome, herby smell. I think that was the first time that I ever thought of hash as a plant product rather than some evil concoction made in a lab somewhere by some post-modern Jekyll.

On the other hand, it was also quite a recognisable smell, and I was worried that someone else might recognise it. I opened a lot of windows and hoped for the best.

'Quinn, it's getting cold in here,' Frank said. 'Will you shut those?'

'But,' I motioned, while whispering forcefully, 'the whole house smells of gear.'

'Yeah, it's good isn't it? Don't you think that it's a lovely smell, Quinn?'

'Well,' I said, taken aback. 'Yeah. It's nice. But what if someone else smells it? What if the warden comes round?'

The warden kept walking past the house. He kept walking right in front of our windows. I shut them.

'Fuck that fat pie-eating cunt,' Frank said, as he passed once again. And that was that.

I went up to my room for a while, to calm my nerves. Frank looked after the Pizza.

Sadly, as he'd already spent the afternoon smoking the rest of the block, Frank's idea of time was not in accordance with the pizza's requirements. By the time he opened the oven door to 'check it out', it would be fair to say that it was the pizza itself that had checked out, and gone up to the great Kinness Fry Bar in the sky. What remained was nothing more than a small, sooty disc with melted cheese in the middle. One charred semicircle looked halfway edible, and Frank set to it. I had the rest.

Fresh off the back of that, and long before it would have any chance to kick in, Frank suggested we hit up some awful homemade bong. I agreed to this, for whatever fool reason I had at the time[*].

Then, after about forty minutes, with the gear coming at me from both directions, we decided to go into town with some of

---

[*] The only other time I'd seen smoke so thick and yellow was when I had tried to reheat a French loaf in the microwave. Within a few seconds it had set itself on fire. You could carry the smoke outside in a bucket. The house stank for a day. The bread, on the other hand, tasted okay, as long as you avoided the parts where it had turned black and shrivelled up.

the DRH crew. There was one man too many for the taxi, so I volunteered to walk it. I didn't think I could handle a taxi ride. It was coming on pretty strong, and I wanted some fresh air. The walk was interesting, although not the most interesting walk of the night.

I got to the Vic, eventually. I felt a little sick. Craig and Frank were playing table football, and I tried to join in but the sheer stimulation of the speed and the movement was too much. I went to the bar to get a drink. A vodka and coke, I decided. Small, sweet, easy to drink. My mouth was dry.

The bar was incredibly orange. The glowing electrical lights hit the creamy walls behind the bar and turned my vision orange. Everything that I looked at, while it retained its original colour, had been tinted with this orange. The bar staff didn't serve me for a long time. I was probably not making eye contact.

I looked around, and the whole place felt like it was outside me, in a brand new way. Outside me, but so was I. Unimportant. Just a part of an evening, no longer the subject. Not even my own protagonist. It is odd to have your whole conception of the world turned on its tail, to the degree that your whole life in front of you suddenly seems to have only the importance of a vibrant mural adorning the wall of a popular student pub with badly painted Scottish celebrities[*].

Eventually I got my drink and the paranoia hit bad while I was waiting for my change. I had an overwhelming urge to run away. I felt like I was about to be caught for some heinous crime and locked away for it. I can't imagine that there would

---

[*] They've painted over the mural now, but I'm still here. I call existential victory.

have been much worse than locking me away in a state like that. I dug in my heels, and collected a handful of coins. I pretended to check them.

'Act normal,' my subconscious was screaming at me 'and you might just get away with it.'

I went back into the next room, and hunched up in a corner, with my vodka and coke within arm's reach. The next thing that I knew, Paedo was talking to me about quake. Paedo's real name was Pedro. I think he had been badly introduced to us in a noisy room, and the name had stuck.

Now he was talking to me about Quake. Paedo still played the original Quake, and don't be deceived; that was almost as old-school then as it would be now. Not many people were still spending five hours a day playing Quake in their rooms at the turn of the millennium. My mouth was dry. I couldn't reply. I took a sip of the mixer.

I tried to dig my feet into the ground and say something, but the room had sloped off into the distance. My eyes watered. My tongue felt heavy in the bottom of my mouth. I started to talk to him, and then stopped in mid sentence. I knew that I hadn't finished speaking, but there was simply no movement in my mouth. A moment later, I had forgotten what I was trying to say.

'Dude,' Paedo said, as he often did, 'You're wasted.'

I was aware of every square millimetre of my thumb and finger skin in contact with my cool glass of vodka coke. My head was tight and felt oppressed. The stimulation from simply talking, moving and breathing was too much. I felt claustrophobic. I could feel the material of my jeans moving against the inside of my legs in a rhythmic timing with my drawn out breaths. Every neuron seemed to be firing at once, and nothing was being filtered out. There was just too much to process.

'Fucked,' I said. 'Going home.'

It was one of the crazier walks of my life[*]. Every sound on the street seemed to be magnified in amplitude and would echo inside my head for just a fraction of a second. I could see perfectly, but the world that I was seeing seemed to be a very long way away, and quite outside of my reach. It was like it was happening somewhere else.

Shadows seemed to move at the periphery of my vision, reminding me of the time that I had stayed awake to see three sunrises in a row. On the last night, I had *seen* things. In the shadows, at the edges of my vision, where nothing was very clear, *things* had been moving. This was even more intense. Where I might once have stopped and wondered if I had seen something in the shadows, now it was writhing and squirming, even when I turned to look directly at it.

Eventually, those things moved out of the shadows. They weren't that terrifying, as it turned out. One of them was a red bike, moving horizontally across the road. I cannot explain how that made sense, but at the time it was perfectly understandable. That was how that bike worked. Why question it?

I had thoughts, as I walked. Deep theological and philosophical musings. They flitted in and out of my mind at massive speed, barely forming themselves into words, often appearing merely as pictures.

---

[*] And I'm known for that.

Answers came, and went as quickly. The thoughts raced, but I couldn't hold on to them, they rushed through me like a river, each with the force of a previously unknown universal truth, vanishing downstream. Like rivers of the mind; never the same, always present, never same. Meaning infusing the least pattern, the least moment, and then gone.

It was like hearing a new a tune as you drift into sleep, and wanting to remember it, but knowing that you have no way to write it down, and that its memory will be gone by morning. I had these thoughts, these *answers*, so it seemed, and I knew that they would all be gone in a split second. I tried to turn one of them into some kind of mantra that I could repeat, and likely remember. I could keep it by repeating it, over, and over.

It's very easy to see why some people feel attuned to God, in that state – or come to believe in some kind of universal, spiritual oneness. But it's not evidence of God's unadorned closeness to humanity. If it shows anything, it shows how many levels must exist between us, and how unsurpassable might be the void. Especially when you're fucked.

I half-ran the rest of the way back to the house, and scribbled the mantra down on the first piece of paper I could find. It was a blue post-it note. Satisfied, I stuck on some music and got into my bed.

The music was incredible. Like nothing I had ever heard, incredible. I listened to music that I'd always listened to and it sounded totally different. It was like I had the world's most selective graphic equaliser in my head. All sorts of different sounds, some of them little more than background noise in the track, became a part of the music. Instruments were all connected and moved in time with each other, moved through each other. I listened to a few random tunes, I listened to a couple of Hendrix tracks, and then – finest of all – I put on all of *OK Computer*. The bass lines passed through the melodies, sweeping the other instruments in and out of the limelight, and I felt at that moment that I had never heard anything so well conceived or created.

I listened to *Media Sift (Through Heart Rises)*. As I listened to *Media Sift*, it never occurred to me how much it would come to represent the whole year in my life, and not just the year, but the act of looking back on it.

with each day and each look back / i remember the voice of young love / and old folks i hear no more / 'till very soon the vision's unsure / i remember arriving home / to old rooms i see no more / 'till very soon it sounds unsure / until the only remnance fades from mind

I fell asleep a little before the end of the CD. When I woke up I was a bit dizzy, but had pretty much recovered. It was mid-afternoon. There was a blue post-it note next to a glass of water. The writing was messy and urgent. The message was surprisingly relaxed.

'Don't worry,' I had written. 'You won't remember any of this in the morning, but it will all still be true.'

Cassie

I never spoke to Cassie. I never heard her voice. I never knew her. I only saw her once, ever, and that was for about ten seconds. I still think about her.

I used to have tea at Darcy Loch's place constantly, and sometimes we'd get some drinks in the evening, too. From all the time I spent with Darcy, you'd have thought something was going on between us. But I remember those days, and it wasn't.

Darcy was just not that appealing. She knew me too well, for one thing. Occasionally, I would still imagine fucking her, but I don't really think that's so unusual. When you don't want something, but you know it's there, sometimes a kind of static builds up. We had that, between us, always. Even at the time, I could tell that Darcy knew what I was thinking in those frozen moments when I spaced out and spent too long following her curves. I think she liked the edge it gave her.

Mostly, though, we drank tea and talked about the things we had in common. We didn't have all that much in common, though, so Darcy used to just blether on as if I was interested in whatever else came into her head, and I did the same, and eventually I realised that's just what people do. Darcy really didn't have any girl friends left, at the start of second year. I reckon I was a nutritional supplement for that, a human vitamin if you will, which is to say that I'm pretty sure that Darcy just pretended I was a girl. This worked surprisingly well, because one of the few things we had in common was Craig and, as far as I can tell, he did the same thing.

So Darcy would have me round for tea, and she'd bitch about her ex-boyfriend, and then talk about food, and not eating food, and going to the gym – all of which were big issues in my life as well, again mostly thanks to the ex-boyfriend. For my part, I got to learn which bits of Cosmopolitan magazine to take seriously, and which bits nobody takes seriously, which is still probably the most valuable object-lesson I've had in sex[*].

We'd sit up in her room and chat because it was, by virtue of being only slighter larger than Pavarotti's coffin, de facto *cosy*, but also because Darcy's flatmates were twisted eldritch abominations of the worst variety. They were not her first choice in flatmates.

All of Darcy's housing plans had fallen through over summer, torn asunder by broken friendships, and she'd taken what she could get in the first week of term. In St. Andrews, what you get if you're looking for accommodation in the first week of term is fucked in the trash pipe.

Darcy paid a King's ransom for a box overlooking the all night garage, with a pair of undead flatmates who ate her food and then left disparaging remarks about its quality though the medium of magnetic fridge poetry.

It was one of that pair of murderously kitsch ghouls who let me in, the day I met Cassie. We didn't stand on ceremony by then, so I never gave it a second thought when Darcy didn't answer the door. Her flatmate waved me inside, all white highlights like the Bride of Hammer Horror. She never said a word to me.

'Thanks,' I said.

She nodded, up the way. I looked at the shadowy staircase.

---

[*] In short, Cosmo is probably a subtle parody masquerading as a garish rag. Failing that insight, the simplest explanation is the best one: it's just a bit shit.

'Right,' I said, hoping that's where Darcy was.

The bedroom door was open, so I knocked casually and stepped into the sunlit space within. Strange eyes met me as I crossed the threshold, deep and green, but what hit me was the contempt. I took a step back.

Cassie was overweight, with milky skin and tired features. She flinched when I moved, her mouth- shape sour with fear and blame. I felt like I'd walked into a wall, it was so strong I was almost dizzy with it.

'Get out!' Darcy said, shooing me like a dog. I hadn't even noticed her, sitting on the bed. 'Go on, now.'

'Uh,' I said, feeling winded. ' Should I wait for you?'

'Just go, fucking go,' Darcy said. 'Get out right now.'

Her silent partner stared me into oblivion. Ghostlike, I faded from the room. The only thing I could feel was my cheeks, burning red. I went back downstairs in a jumble, and fell out of the door. I sat on the steps outside for a couple of minutes, feeling rejected and indignant.

When I got back to Fife Park, the Randoms were playing Monopoly in Gowan's room, with Frank. Frank was out, but wouldn't give his share of the money back to the bank, which was causing a minor financial crisis. I sat on Gowan's bed. It was too late to join, but they passed round the cider. Frank gave me a thousand pound note.

'You look like you need cheering up,' he said. 'Don't spend it all at once.'

The War of the Randoms

Noises came from downstairs. Sometimes they were loud, and violent. There were sounds of banging, clattering, thumping, laughter, screams, and the odd distinguishable obscenity. As our friendship with the Randoms still hung by a thread, we feared the worst.

The Randoms were Gowan Crimp, William Pace and Dylan Tellgood.

By November, we had started to use these names, instead of just calling them the Randoms and, in kind, they had stopped ignoring us and introduced themselves properly.

Gowan was a small, athletic guy, who was always on the lookout for a good time. He had round cheeks, boyish, appealing looks – which have never really left him – and an easy, comfortable manner. He had a roguishly casual attitude to sex, which served him well and infuriated those of us who took sex very seriously indeed and consequently weren't getting any.

Will was a lithe and good looking blonde guy, with an eighty quid haircut. He went home every weekend in his decrepit Golf to ride horses and visit a girlfriend who we never met. It had been a High School romance, and her half of it still was, either because she was inappropriately young, or desperately re-sitting her way out of the Sixth Form. Will didn't drink with us often but, when he did, he used to get very drunk, very quickly. Getting him home was always a nightmare, partly because he had a penchant for exposing himself, but mostly because if he came across anything taller than himself he'd climb it and refuse to come down until morning.

I confronted Gowan about the noises at one point, but he countered that noises also came from upstairs, that he often heard people screaming at Americans, and that he was perpetually disturbed by what sounded like something being dragged across the ceiling of his room late at night. He insinuated that it might have been something *awful*. I didn't pursue the matter.

Usually the disturbances were short-lived in any case, so much so that none of us had made it down in time to see whatever was causing them. Usually the only signs of trouble were minor surface damage. There was a hole in Gowan's door one day, for example, and then a slightly larger hole in Will's the next.

One night the noises started and didn't die down, so I was nominated to investigate. As I got to the bottom of the stairs, I was almost knocked off my feet by Gowan rushing into the house with his arms full of damp and fusty autumnal leaves. He was in hot pursuit of Will, who managed to shut his bedroom door just too late to stop the first barrage of dirty brown leaves from entering in his wake.

The kitchen was in a state. It looked like people had been throwing things at each other. Arguably that wasn't unusual, although to the trained eye there was definitely something amiss. Outside the house, the damage went further. Will's Volkswagen had been attacked with peaches, eggs and flour. At that time, tinned peaches were down to such an unreasonably low price that they were cheap enough to use as either a light snack or as light artillery.

'Grab some eggs!' Gowan encouraged me, running into the kitchen. 'There's still a few clean spots on Will's car!'

'No,' Will called, holding him down, 'go and get some leaves, and put them in Gowan's bed...'

'I was just coming downstairs for a yoghurt,' I lied.

'That'll do!' Gowan said, feverishly. 'Throw it over the windscreen.'

The struggle continued as I went upstairs, yoghurt in hand, to report back to Frank and Craig. They both pronounced the Randoms insane, which certainly seemed possible. I don't know what Craig thought about that, but I think Frank rather viewed it as a challenge.

After it became clear that Gowan and Will were all kinds of trouble, Frank made easy headway with them. Next time they went crazy, he was right there with them, albeit principally in an advisory capacity. Crazy wasn't worth making too much of an effort over in Frank's book.

'Use the chair!' he said, when Will locked himself in his room.

Gowan pounded another hole in Will's door with a chair leg.

'Pour water in his bed,' he advised Will, after Gowan had finally passed out.

'He'll have a fucking heart attack if I pour cold water over him,' Will objected.

'Hmm,' Frank said, a trace of disappointment in his voice. 'I'm almost sure that won't happen.'

Will went to get a bucket.

That was the beginning of the end. After Frank switched sides, there was no point trying to keep the house in order, and even Craig let himself go a bit. The next week, while making pancakes, we had what began as a food-fight.

It was just a minor ruckus, started when Craig, out of curiosity, poured cocoa powder into the mixing bowl. I poured one into the pan, but it didn't cook right. So we grabbed a few handfuls of stodgy half-cooked mix, and threw them at each other. Also at the ceiling because, remarkably, they didn't come down again. The fight left the kitchen, and pretty quickly escalated into something more.

Sometimes we were all in it together. At one point, we poured several litres of water downstairs, just to see what it would look like[*].

But then sometimes it was a battle. I took it like a man when Frank threw water over the balcony at me, but I hid in the downstairs bathroom when the bottles it had been in came down, too. They were followed by soap powder, a few bathroom copies of *The Saint,* some cardboard and a thick woolly blanket.

I was in the bathroom for quite a long time. Craig danced about on the rug madly, working everything into a lather. We left everything exactly where it was when we went to bed.

---

[*] Like a wet Slinky.

The Crack of McWinslow

Euan McWinslow was a damn contradiction. He was a thoroughly right wing conservative, who loved American surf punk and smoking weed. He started University at sixteen, but carried himself like a middle aged banker. He had a weak constitution[*], pale skin and strawberry hair, but he partied harder and longer than anyone else I knew, and threw himself into one extreme beach sport after another. One night I saw him ad lib a six minute rap about a plush toy lizard[†]. Later he spent two hours explaining rent control, with no noticeable dip in enthusiasm.

We knew Euan from New Hall, but he went to Gatty when we went to Fife Park; same shit, different end of town. We knew Euan well enough to like him, and also well enough to know that his dial-to-eleven speaker system was better off at the other end of town. I visited maybe twice all year. True to form he lived in a punk rock house, where he studied economics fastidiously.

The other thing about Euan that I remember vividly, is that Darcy Loch fell for him in a big way.

'How *hot* is Euan?' she asked me, one day. 'Those pecs are devastating, and his ass is like some kind of dimpled rock formation.'

That was the first I knew of it. It did not please me to consider Euan in this fresh new light.

---

[*] For Euan, vomiting was a form of punctuation.
[†] The inimitable 'Gecko Superstar'.

'Yeah,' I said. 'We're probably not going to find a lot of common ground here.'

'Oh come on, it's not like you can't tell who's the best looking amongst your friends.'

'I *can* tell,' I said. 'But I don't. Just like I don't check out their baloney at the froth-trough. This is the way of things.'

'I bet you do, sometimes,' she said.

'You know nothing of men.'

'Fine,' she grumped. 'I was just saying.'

'He's nice,' I conceded. 'You could do worse. Don't mention his rocky Greco-Roman arse dimples again.'

'I didn't say Greco-Roman.'

'Hmm,' I said. 'I'm almost sure you did.'

'Do you think he's too young for me?'

'Fuck, you're the one who talks about maturity. Whatever.'

'He doesn't seem too young, but then sometimes he does. He's like, forty going on seventeen.'

'You better like loud music something chronic. That's the worst I can say.'

'He's *sooo hawt*. That party we had last week.'

'The Gecko Party,' I said.

'You could feel the tension.'

'Huh,' I said.

It was a *huh* moment. I guess I thought we had the corner on sexual tension. But, obviously, ours was the back burner kind.

'Like, all electricity and hotness, and wow!'

'I don't think I know that feeling,' I said; a half truth.

'I almost ripped the pants off him right there,' she said. Then she said it again.

'Huh,' I said.

I could sense the frustration in her voice. And I was winded by my own bilious jealousy.

'I don't care,' I said. Out loud, but to myself. Firmly. 'I don't care. It's none of my business.'

'What, you don't think I should?'

'No,' I said, 'I think he's into you. It's all good.'

'Well, I didn't mean to make things all weird...'

'No,' I said.

'If it's because he's your friend or something,' she started.

'No,' I said. 'Why does everybody think that matters?'

'Doesn't it?'

'I guess. Look, though. He's a good one. You'll have fun.'

'You think it's probably just a thing?'

'Everything's just a thing.'

'I mean, you think he'd see it as just fun?'

'I don't know. I guess it depends how you play it.'

'Fine,' she said. 'I get it. You don't want to talk about it.'

'No, it's not that. It's just... are *we* alright? Are we properly friends?'

'Totally,' she said. 'Really good friends.' Her voice went up a pitch, frank with worry. 'Why? What's wrong?'

'No, we're fine,' I said. 'If you say so, we're fine. There's nothing wrong. Only I just don't know what happened, you know, the other week.'

She took a deep breath.

'Cassie,' she said.

'That her name?'

'Yeah.'

'What did I do to deserve that?'

'Sorry I was a bitch,' she said. 'You just had to go is all, and I didn't know how else to say it so you would.'

'Yeah, fine,' I said. 'You were a bitch. But I was talking about her.'

'Quinn,' she said.

'Did you even see the way she looked at me? It was like she wanted me to die.'

'Quinn, she's not well.'

'As in 'mentally fucking ill' not well.'

'Yes.'

'Oh,' I said. 'I was just kidding around.'

'She has trust issues with men. That's all you need to know.'

'At last someone thinks I'm a fucking man,' I said.

'Jesus, Quinn!'

'Well,' I said. 'I fail to see how it's my problem.'

'It's not your problem, but have a bit of human compassion. You're being a prick.'

'OK, well how should I be about it?'

'Patient,' she said. 'Well, I have to be patient. You have to be gone, and that's just how it is.'

'What did I ever do that she gets to decide when I go?'

'Nothing. But don't bother playing the discrimination card, here, Quinn. You don't fit the demographic.'

'Oh, so I can't feel bad about it, now, either.'

'Get over yourself, Quinn. Really.'

'Whatever.'

Darcy looked at me. Bit her lip. Decided to spill the beans.

'When she was younger, every man she knew abused her. All of them, seriously. Her whole family. I'm not going to talk about how. I shouldn't even be telling you this.'

'Shit,' I said.

I had probably figured it was something whiny and inner-child up to that point, because I remember the sinking, evil feeling I got when Darcy opened up.

'She got 'rescued', when she was twelve. I've been looking out for her a bit this year. But it's hard fucking going, and you're making it harder.'

'Fuck.'

I rubbed my forehead with my fingertips.

'She's not ever getting better, is she?' I realised.

'It's really not about better.'

'Sorry,' I said. 'Fuck.'

'Puts things into perspective.'

'I don't know. I don't know where it even fits in.'

'You're lucky,' she said. 'Even though you don't know a thing about anything. I mean, honestly, not a thing. Sometimes I think you're a blank slate.'

'I'm better at some things than others,' I said.

'Yeah.'

We just sat there in silence after that. I don't know how she felt, but it wasn't a deliberate act of respect or gravity that kept me quiet. I would have talked, if I could. I would have gone right on and rated every one of my male friends by buttock firmness rather that sit there in silence. It just didn't seem like there was anything you could follow it up with that wouldn't be out of place.

And I remember thinking that it would probably be hours before I could tell another stupid joke, or make some comment about boobs. And I remember thinking 'Time will fix this awkward moment just fine. But some people are broken.' And there were a million things I didn't think. There could have been a neon sign, and I would have missed it, but I never even wondered how Darcy met Cassie, or where.

Wallow Man

Craig, at about this time, announced his intention to move out. I don't know which part of it all that he didn't like. It might have been the mess. It might have been the noise (the walls were made of cardboard after all). It might have been the relative lack of creature comforts. It might have been a single incident, like the time that Frank pinned raw fish fingers to the kitchen noticeboard.

He might have been hurt by my burgeoning friendship with Darcy, or just nonplussed enough to leave. He certainly never liked his room, although he had landed one on the sunny side.

We didn't really want Craig to move out. Frank, of course, didn't *seem* to give a shit, but I asked Craig to stay on behalf of both of us. Fife Park didn't tolerate empty rooms for long, and the overseas income of Semester II was fast approaching.

'We'll get some random German called Helmut!' I pleaded.

But Craig went to see the warden, all the same; that corpulent pie-muncher Dorian Tombs. Never before, in all my experience, had such a sour faced man, in charge of a place of so little significance, approached any task with such great pomp. Dorian Tombs was king of the molehill.

The first time that the pie-muncher came around to see us personally was less than a week after the washing powder fiasco. This was no coincidence. The cleaning staff came around every fortnight and made themselves tea in our kitchen. They never said a word to us, or cleaned anything for that matter. However, they made a point of reporting all house discrepancies back to the warden, like some kind of ugly, pensionable, secret police force.

Dorian came around while Craig was in the shower. The blanket, newspaper, and soggy, frothy, washing powder mix still festered outside the door. That week particularly stands out in my memory; I recall leaping over the caustic mess every morning and scrambling for safety. Craig, of course, wore his flip flops into the shower and foresaw no difficulties on that particular morning. He was the only person in the house, at the time.

Tombs cased the joint, no doubt, before knocking at the door of the bathroom. Craig ignored him, for a while. The knocking grew more insistent, so he called out:

'Fuck off!'

Dorian Tombs did not fuck off. Dorian Tombs kept knocking.

Craig eventually got out of the shower, threw a towel around his waist, and opened the door. He found himself looking into Dorian's shiny, bald pate. He probably saw the future, or at least part of what it held.

'Oh,' said Craig. Then I rather suspect that he asked something along the lines of 'Can I help you?'

I doubt, quite seriously, that he told him to 'fuck off' again.

Dorian had a Polaroid camera hanging around his neck. He was a great collector of 'evidence.'

'Only perverts have Polaroid cameras,' Frank said, later.

I think that there's a lot of truth in that. Polaroid spent a lot of money in the eighties trying to dissociate themselves from the pervert image. They used to sell on the merit of 'fun' and 'convenience'. They didn't, of course, distance themselves from the perverts completely. There's a lot of money in perverts; there's a lot of them around[*].

At any rate, I can say from experience that Dorian Tombs never exuded an air of fun or convenience. It was quite simply not his way. He led Craig into the kitchen, and waved around with his hand.

'You live like pigs,' he told him.

'Yes,' Craig said. 'I'm planning to move out. I've already been to see you about it.'

That took the wind out of his sails.

'Why is there food on the ceiling?' Dorian asked, after a long pause.

That took the wind out of Craig's sails, and the fat bastard left without saying much else. There were no threats but from then on we were marked men.

---

[*] It was an interesting development that Polaroid had to pull out of their main market when digital cameras took off, but it wasn't the most interesting development I've seen, thanks to Polaroid.

Constitutional

In theory, the New Hall Christmas party was a really decent night out. Like good empiricists, we laboured to revise that theory to meet the available facts; namely that it was a decent night out for people who weren't us. In the first year, Frank and Mart drank four bottles of white wine between them before setting off and respectively puked on the bus, and sat in puke on the bus – and not as unrelated incidents, I might add. In the second year, I made my final catastrophic attempt to romance Ella, and then risked death to forget it. I also trod in deer shit, which was really not on the radar at the start of the evening.

The party was annually hosted at a bona fide, genuine nightclub called Enigma, although the real mystery was why anyone would want to spend a night in the scary part of Dundee[*]. After the buses pulled up, a bunch of wasted local kids hurled abuse at us and, later, chips. Graffiti on the dirty bricks of the nightclub itself depicted a sex act that, despite close to two decades of unfettered internet access, I have still never seen reproduced in porn.

That night I was wearing a flamboyant and ill-chosen shirt, the entire merits of which consisted in its being of, at least in part, a festive colour. I was also wearing a 'Jingle Bells' musical tie, which must have been the result of a gentlemanly wager of some sort because even at that point in my life I wouldn't have stooped so close to a total suicide of dignity. It had a little Santa with flashing red LED eyes.

---

[*] Which is all of it.

I don't know why I was asking Ella out again. I wish I could remember, because it seemed mostly reasonable at the time. It was all undone in the execution, of course: I'd come to the conclusion that if it wasn't going to happen with the aid of mistletoe, then it wasn't going to happen at all. With hindsight applied, the cautious application of Occam's Razor might have saved me some time, as well as the fifty pence I spent on a plastic sprig of New Hall committee's party-approved mistletoe substitute.

The club was dark, but bright with it. Neon nights glared into the smoky air. Could have been dry ice, probably it was just cigarettes. It was all gaudy and cyberpunk, and I guess it felt like somewhere you could have a good time.

'I've got a tattoo!' Ella said, when I sat next to her.

'I've got a scar under my eye,' I said.

'That's not the same.'

'I guess not.'

'Do you want to see it?'

'OK,' I said. 'Did it hurt?'

She leaned forwards, and brushed her long hair to one side. Her low back dress showed it off, a tiny thing on her left shoulder blade.

'A bit. I got it done with my friend, in Glasgow. She had an ankle one. That was *really* sore.'

'Why the butterfly?'

'I just liked it. It was in the book.'

'Huh,' I said.

111

'What's up? You look sick.'

'I was going to ask...' I said.

'Yeah?'

'Uh, I have this mistletoe,' I said, words falling out of me. 'If I hold it above your head, would you kiss me?'

'No,' she said, firmly.

She held up a hand. It called her No, and raised it an additional Stop Right There.

'Huh,' I said, again.

I was mostly surprised. I really don't know what I expected. It just seemed kind of unsporting to say no to mistletoe. I pushed the cheap sprig into her hand, and stared up at the ceiling, as if for inspiration. There was no mistletoe up there amongst flashing lights and ventilation pipes.

'Well that's going to be embarrassing in the morning.'

She nodded.

'I won't ask you again,' I said.

'OK.'

'Look,' I said. 'This is the only time you've never had anything to say to me. I don't want to make it like this. Honestly.'

She got up. Hovered awkwardly for a second. I looked at the floor, shook my head. When I finished my bottle I went to the bar. Mart was there.

'Buy me a beer,' I told him. 'It has not been a good day for the Empire.'

He did. He's a generous sort when he's pissed. I bought him one back, and then a couple more to tide us over.

'Double-fisting,' Mart said, with a grin. 'The gentleman's alternative to sexual success.'

'You saw that, then?' I asked him.

'Saw what?'

I raised a bottle, and clinked it with one of his.

'I'm going to drink till I can see the funny side of that.'

My next memory, which could be from hours later, is of sitting at a little round coffee table full of empty bottles, by myself, on a stain-cushioned horseshoe bench. Almost by myself: Sandy Bertrando was sitting five feet away, looking like I felt and for some reason that I will never know, cradling my musical tie to his ear and repeatedly tormenting himself with its festive banshee death wail[*]. I watched with a kind of distracted fascination. Santa's demon eyes glared back at me.

Looking back over to the bar, I saw Ella getting chatted up by one of our local sports stars. He was leaning in. She was responding well. I felt a bitter, helpless surge of jealousy. He put his hand on her shoulder, she touched her mouth. I kicked the coffee table, hard, and it overturned, scattering bottles and beer dregs over the sticky carpet. It was time to leave.

When I got outside, there were no buses waiting. A bunch of students were milling at the local kebab shop. I walked past them. There would be other buses.

I walked downhill a few blocks, until I reached the bank of the Tay. There was a huge, old fashioned boat moored up:

---

[*] a.k.a. Season's Greeting.

Discovery. I didn't know which way I was going at that point, but straight on looked wet and I wasn't going back.

I tried to follow the water towards the bridge because I figured that as long as I was always walking towards it then I couldn't help but get there eventually. I guess the same thought applied to Fife Park in a wider sense. I didn't know how I was getting back at that point. There was no plan. There was just the anti-plan that was putting distance between myself and that fucking club.

I couldn't follow the water. There were obstacles in my path. There were fences, buildings, passes, flights of stairs, shopping centres which were closed past eight in the evening. I remember walking down a long dark corridor which was most decidedly indoors in some manner that I don't quite understand. I remember shimmying along a thin pipe. Eventually I got to the Tay Bridge.

There was a manned tollbooth back then. Cars were passing on either side. I walked up to the booth, and asked if there was some way to cross on foot. There was, in the form of a small service path running between the lanes of traffic with safety barriers on either side. I patiently waited at the booth as an old geezer was hailed on some kind of two way radio. A few moments later, I saw him huffing out of a terminal over the road.

The barrier had to be opened with a key. I remember vaguely hoping that this wouldn't be an issue once I reached the other side of the bridge. The guy unlocking the gate challenged me, half-heartedly.

'I live on the other side of it,' I told him. 'And I want to go home.'

I don't know why he opened the gate and let me cross, but he did. Maybe there's some legal right of way – even if you're a man in just his shirt sleeves in the middle of December, pissed out of his mind, ranting, stumbling, and barely able to speak. Also, I guess it's always possible they thought I was a local.

As I walked out onto the bridge – in fact, at the very moment that the gate closed behind me – I felt a rush of cold wind as the first returning bus passed me. It was full of drunk students. It looked like the party was still going on inside, glowing with energy, and pressing a warm, yellow luminance into the darkness. It was very fucking cold when that bus was out of sight. I finally realised, in the light of new and overwhelming evidence, that I was not going to get home before my fellow partygoers. After the bus, there was no more traffic on the bridge for minutes on end. It was just me, stumbling along, bouncing off the rails on either side of me, and never seeming to get any closer to the other side, partly because it is a fucking long bridge and one bit of it looks pretty much like another, and partly because I was walking sideways as often as forwards.

Periodically there were signs above my head with the number of the Bridge Services Department emblazoned across them. I wanted to turn back, but felt that I must be closer to the other side. I don't know at what point that stopped being wishful thinking. It never occurred to me then that crossing the bridge would be the shortest part of the journey.

I cannot stress enough how fucking freezing I was. It was not a thick shirt that I was wearing and as it turns out, warm colours aren't, particularly. I didn't even have my tie. Sandy was probably still cradling it, on the bus, halfway back to St. Andrews. All the way back maybe. He could have been asleep by then.

It wasn't much warmer when I finally reached the other side, but there was less wind. There was, thankfully, no gate at the other end. There would have been no one to open it. I had to crawl up a gigantic sloped embankment to find the road again. I muddied my jeans falling on my knees. I muddied my hands picking myself back up. I was determined. I walked across the middle of a large roundabout.

It was already too late to really be a decision by then, but that was when I decided, in a fool state, that I would get Ella out of my system once and for all by walking back, and thinking things over. There was all the time in the world. I'm sure I did my share of thinking, but I don't remember a whit of it. I do remember gritting my teeth to stop them banging off each other.

I walked along embankments where the road had embankments. Sometimes they were muddy, and sometimes they were hard to walk on because of hidden stones or thick tufts of grass. Often I walked straight down the middle of the road. I tried to stay between the lanes. Sometimes I walked down the middle of those, too. I kept my ears pricked up for traffic, but there was precious little of it. I was more afraid than comforted when it passed. I felt safer alone, but then I was afraid of the dark. Quite afraid, I remember. There were sometimes animal noises, lowing and barking, the sound of the countryside, which made me feel as small as the dark is large. I was in the middle of it, miles and miles into the middle of it, and there was nothing to do but try and get out of it.

The first time I needed a piss, I went off-road. I walked up a little hillside. At the top was a small wooded section. It was extremely foreboding, but once again I refused to turn back. I pissed against a tree with massive satisfaction.

When I turned around, I heard something else moving.

'Oh shitting fuck,' I said.

It heard me, and whatever it was broke into a run. I couldn't tell if it was coming towards me or running away.

'Fucking fuck me.' It was a whimper.

My throat closed up and my heart lurched. But there was nothing to do about it. I was terrified of something in the dark, and unlike in a nightmare it was *really* there, only I couldn't see it.

The running noise got quieter. I stood in the same spot until I couldn't hear anything but rustling leaves. It was probably a deer, because when I came out of the other side of the wood, I trod in shit and I'm almost certain it wasn't my own. There were several large piles of it, and I reckon I found them all. I swore a lot, and looked at the stars. I carried on walking.

The road never seemed to change, but the night was getting old. Sometimes I half fell asleep, but I was always walking when I opened my eyes. I remember stopping at the roadside, and wondering whether I should lay down. I started to feel cold right into my bones, and my whole body jolted with it, and so I ran until I warmed up. I don't know how much running I did. I've never really been able to run. Next time I had to piss, I just did it in the road. There was no fucker around for miles.

I could just about read the road signs as I reached Leuchars. I took a wrong turn, and I thought that I was walking through the airbase, but it was just chain link fences on either side of me. I hit the right road after the train station, on the way into Guardbridge. I knew those roads, and knew St. Andrews was only seven miles further down them. That made it seem close. The sky grew gradually lighter, and traffic picked up.

The last hour was the longest. The sky went from inky to mild grey down the long road into St. Andrews. I could see the pattern of lights marking the Golf Hotel for near an hour before I reached it. One of my hips hurt. It felt like it was grinding in the socket.

I was sobering up, and starting to see things for what they were. The temptation to try and hail one of the passing cars grew into an urge. But by that time, it was a journey almost done. I had started to feel kind of good about things. I wanted to finish the walk, and be able to say that I had walked it. I didn't particularly want to say that I had gotten into some shitty red Fiesta on the last leg of the journey.

Eventually I was opposite the Golf Hotel, back in St. Andrews, and suddenly the walk was just a walk from the Golf Hotel to Fife Park, and not an insurmountable goal. I walked down the back path, behind New Hall, and into Fife Park. I had a few glasses of water in the kitchen from an unrinsed glass as the sun blazed into my eyes through the window. It was only just a fraction above the horizon and it had turned the ugly walls of the kitchen bright orange. I could feel the warmth of the sun on my chest, and its cool absence on my back. Ella seemed a million miles away, at the end of a tunnel. So did the whole of the night.

'Is that you Quinine?' I heard Frank call, as I reached the door to my room.

Frank is the only person who calls me by my full first name, pronouncing it like *Kwin-in*.

'Leave me the fuck alone,' I said. I went to my bed.

The next afternoon, when I woke up, I felt stupid. But also slightly smug. The world felt more like a place I was in than it had the night before. I walked from town to town – a seemingly impossible feat. I had never walked from one large town to another before. I'd never done it by day, let alone by night; never even biked it. Towns and cities have always seemed like separate worlds that can only be reached along thin interconnecting roads, by rocket-fuelled modes of automotive transport. It comforts me, even now, to think that it can still be done. It calms me to know that everywhere is somewhere you can walk, give or take. It is *so* comforting to think that if all the world's fuel ever runs out, I won't find myself stuck for the rest of my life in, say, Hull.

The Dudes

Craig moved out after the first semester. For some reason or other, after Craig moved out, the house matured into a loafer's paradise. Our last vestigial standards went the way of the dodo: the kitchen stopped getting cleaned at all, drunken people messed things up and sober people left the mess where it was. It was an odd situation because I swear Craig never washed up more than twice in the whole time he was in Fife Park, but the kitchen was always cleaner when he was there.

They don't like wasting space at Residential Services; ask the bunk-bed generation, who had to study at their shared desk in shifts and still find enough time to cry themselves to sleep. We all understood that we'd get a replacement housemate. We still joked that we'd get a German exchange student called Helmut.

None of us guessed that he would be American, even though that was probably the most obvious option. St. Andrews has a permanent neon-lit olive branch at the other side of the pond, and the place itself was always highly Americanised, with the golf, Semesters, and the perpetual stream of tourists. Accordingly, there's an influx of single-semester exchange students who bubble into St. Andrews at the beginning of February. We got Brad. We called him Helmut, behind his back.

Brad was a huge American, from Vermont. He had slightly thinning, curly, strawberry-blonde hair, and looked like he could bench a Buick. I don't know how old he was, but he looked rugged enough that I reckon you could have cut him in half and counted the rings. He sported a stubbly ginger beard most of the time. He used to go out every day for runs, and would wear a bandana when he exercised. He used to go to the gym, which made him as far removed from, say, Frank McQueen as some of the higher primates.

He also routinely spent an hour in the bathroom taking a shit and reading the papers. The first time he did it, and the mellow stink wafted over the stairwell and infused the house with the aroma of poo, we all thought that something had gone seriously wrong.

'Dude, I think Brad shat himself to death,' I announced. Frank was opening a can of tomato soup.

'Isn't it amazing,' Frank began, 'how a tin of tomato soup fits exactly into one of these bowls?' He carefully manoeuvred the rim-full bowl into the microwave and then threw a couple of slices of bread into the toaster.

'So what's it like upstairs with Helmut?' Gowan asked[*].

'Well, not very pleasant precisely right now. But, ah... he seems okay. Just different, maybe. He doesn't understand anything I say. We're kind of talking at cross-purposes. You know he leaves the door open when he takes a shit?'

'Right open?'

'Ajar. Just enough to let things circulate. But he leaves his bedroom door open when he's naked.[†]'

---

[*] We even managed to convince Will that he was actually called Helmut, for the first three days.

[†] Brad hadn't been entirely in the buff when I had walked in on him, but it was still a shock. He was unpacking his suitcase, in a pair of boxers. Brad had brought four books with him and little else it seemed. Three were guides to Scotland, including some awful-looking A-Z, and the last was Trainspotting.

Just as the microwave pinged ready, none other than Brad walked into the room, evidently on a quest for a manly greeting of some sort. He chose Frank.

It should be said that Brad's greetings were typically rugged and outdoorsy, with just a twist of frat boy, and therefore notable not least for their latent homoeroticism. Forewarned, this could have been a stimulating moment of pure cultural exchange. Frank never even saw it coming.

I was in a fortunate position, insomuch as that I could not only see Brad draw back his arm and swing it round in an exaggerated motion, before finally grabbing a hold of Frank's derriere with a raucous slap, but that I could also see McQueen's face, the picture of which will remain with me forever.

'Hey, man,' Brad said.

Frank was gingerly holding a bowl of bubbling soup, which was full enough that any motion whatever might have caused a burning spillage of hot tomato lava. He didn't move an inch, in fact, but you could see in his eyes the exact moment at which Brad's beefy paw impacted with his rump.

It was the look of an angry bull, but also the look of a frightened rabbit. It was the classic eyes-wide look of a cartoon animal who, forgetting himself, has just run off the edge of a cliff and is only too late realising the implications of this. Most of all, it was the look of a big hairy man, with another big hairy man's hand on his arse, shocked out of his skin, and yet desperate not to spill boiling soup over himself.

'I'm off into town, guys,' Brad told us, leisurely removing his hand. 'We'll be drinking in Lafferty's if you boys want to catch up with us later.' And with that, he was gone.

There was an actual point at which you heard Frank start to breathe again.

'Did you see that?' he whispered. 'Right on my arse? And, I mean, I'm not exactly a small man. There's a lot of arse to get hold of.'

'Well, he got most of it, mate.'

'Did you see *that*? Did you see it?' Frank kept asking over and over, in a small voice.

'I'll skin up,' I consoled him.

It was all he could do to muster a subdued 'mumble-mumble-something... Eggman.'

The Americans in St. Andrews usually stick together, the exchange students almost exclusively, and Brad was no exception. He rooted out a posse within hours of his arrival and, from then on, they were his crew.

We dubbed them 'The Dudes', and romanticised their better points. They, above all other punters, were truly Random.

We hung out with them a few times, but to little avail. If Brad had arrived speaking only Japanese, we would have found more things in common. Sadly, our apparently shared language seemed to be the greatest barrier to communication. We assumed at the time that we were using it to the same ends, but I think we were mistakenly taking that for granted.

Thank fuck for Dylan; he came into his own when the Dudes arrived. It was as if he'd been born in their midst. He could speak the dialect effortlessly, and we'd look to him for occasional guidance and translation. He even shrugged off his usual reserve and made out with one of them in the Vic one night.

'She said that I was sick,' he said. 'That's a good thing.'

The rest of us were hopeless. In conversation there was always the feeling that we didn't quite understand each other, signalled by an array of awkward pauses, and trailing sentences. I got the impression after chatting with Brad that almost every aspect of our worldview was irreconcilable; that we were fixed in totally different paradigms; and that there was no way we could ever hope to communicate frankly. I've spent a lot more time with Americans since then, and I have nothing to add to this but my gratitude. Life would be a lot less fun if we were all on the same page.

Of course, alcohol being the leveller that it is, we got on famously if we ever made it out of the house. For the most part, they took their ales a lot better than I had expected, mainly because they were so big. Shots were another matter.

It wasn't just Brad – most of the Americans, the lads at any rate, were gigantic. I don't mean that they were fat; I mean that they had the physical build of redwood trees. Big 'Bear' Pete, for example, was an immense man and as solid as a mountain. He was one of Brad's better friends and we often saw him around the house. We got on with him pretty well in the scheme of things. Brad and Pete made 'Scotch Pies' together one night, and we all had a beer and a laugh.

Pete used to wear a shaggy red and black plaid jacket that made him look like a lumberjack. He had massive amounts of scruffy dark hair and also sported a thick, close-trimmed beard. Pete was fucking *built*. When you call a Scottish guy 'built', you tend to mean that he can swallow more than his fair share of pints, swing his full weight, and has probably got no neck.

Pete was built in quite a different sense – he looked like he had been manually constructed out of industrial materials. He was all torso and no gut; a genuine Desperate Dan. Dylan suggested that it was to do with the amount of hormones they inject into cattle in the States. There was no hard science backing that up, but you could just imagine that Pete was seething with bovine power.

It might have been the 'Scotch Pie' night that most of Fife Park 7 went out on the town with Brad and Pete. The two Dudes, still in a perverse kind of tourist mode, had bought a decent bottle of Scotch that Bear Pete was carrying around in his lumber-jacket. On him, it made no more of a bulge than a deck of fags on any other man.

When we were all pretty inebriated, we went out to the union and played drinking games for an hour or two. It wasn't normal for us to play drinking games when we were out, although we'd done it a few times in first year, but it gave us a common purpose and an opportunity to get pissed up with the Dudes, which was always welcome. The plan was to eventually meet with yet more Dudes who, we were assured, had a late-night housewarming on the cards and we'd wangled invites on the side.

I don't quite remember the rules of the game we played in the union, but it was something to do with flipping a coin from your fingertips into a pint glass, and then having to drink, or not to drink, or something to that effect. I do remember that Pete's hands were so big that he didn't so much have to flip the coin as merely drop it into the pint glass. This would have put him at an unfair advantage, but for the fact that he was already so fucked that he missed the rim of the glass more often than not. Brad had huge hands too, as we knew only too well, but his coordination was also insufficient for victory.

We got through a few pints that way and then Pete downed a fresh pint in Olympic time, just because we were ready to leave and all assumed that he couldn't do it. Every one of us was in a rare state by the time we left.

On the way out to the Badlands, the Dudes kept pulling out their whisky and chugging away at it, offering us a couple of swigs which we accepted in the name of friendship. By the time we made it to the top of Bridge Street, Pete and Brad were leaning on each other for support, and Frank was babbling on incoherently about being out with the Dudes.

'Hanging with the Dudes!' he shouted, to no-one in particular.

Enthused by this, Brad and Pete momentarily gained enough energy to high-five each other and jump around a bit. The effect of this was not lost on McQueen, who immediately demanded to know, amongst other things, 'Who's the man?'

Once again, the Dudes were briefly impassioned, leaping into the air and shouting out such delirious non-sequiturs as 'Yeah,' and 'Alright, man.'

After inciting them to kick a few wheelie bins and traffic cones that were temporarily in place on Bell Street, Frank fell back a few steps and lit a cigarette. Pete and Brad once again fell into each other's arms, for support.

'Keeping it real!' Frank called out, experimentally. Again, the dudes jumped, swung and kicked out at various inanimate objects before winding down.

After that, McQueen didn't even bother to make the effort. Satisfied with his new found control, he dropped to a slower pace, keeping ten feet behind the Dudes and proffering more random, inane, sentiments whenever it suited him.

'C'mon! Hanging with the *Dudes!*'

'Who's the man?' Brad demanded at one point, catching the rest of us off guard.

'You're the man,' Frank offered, immediately.

'Yes, definitely you,' I ventured.

'C'mon!' Frank called out, grinning as they flailed and danced. 'Keeping it real.'

The Dude-flat was on Nelson Street; a group of fresh exchange students had rented a private place out, instead of plumping for a simple university residence. It was a typically self-motivated move on the part of the Dudes. If there is one thing I admire about Americans in general, it's their willingness to have things their own way, and not merely settle for the serving suggestion[*].

It was a decent house as well, not the typical student flat. There were screen doors in the dining room, plush sofas and a coffee

---

[*] Although there's a damn fine line between confidently asking for something and sincerely believing that you deserve to get it.

table in the lounge, and a hardwood fitted kitchen with the kind of integrated dishwasher that serves to highlight the futility of middle class success. It had an overflowing fruit basket, to which we were entreated to help ourselves by various Dudes.

There were five or six of them in the house, but I don't remember any names. Bryan, perhaps, was a short cropped Dude and instigator of the party, and there was a girl with frizzy black hair and a remarkably square jaw called Sam, or Sharon, who was Pete's first target.

Pete immediately and systematically began victimising the occupants of the lounge. He was a restless drunk and wasn't happy in an empty chair. Instead he sprawled anywhere that somebody else was trying to sit, clambering on top of them, his crushing weight suffocating whomever was beneath him.

When they had stopped moving, or in some cases breathing, he'd jump to his feet and pick a new playmate, only to crush them half to death as well, all the while laughing, tickling, jabbing and poking at them with enough force to crack a rib. He made a great drunk, it has to be said.

On the strength of Pete's vitality, we soon found out what kind of a party it was: it was the kind that wasn't. Some of Bryan's flatmates were already objecting, particularly the flattened ones in the lounge and a ratty-faced studious Dudette who seemed to hate everybody and lived on her own upstairs.

'I don't know why you're even here,' she said. 'But can you fucking keep it down?'

As a matter of fact, nobody knew why we were there, which was in equal parts amusing and concerning. Stripped of the context of an invitation, it appeared to all intents and purposes that we had turned up at a random household in the middle of the night and started assaulting people.

Eventually somebody came into the room and took Pete away, leading him by the hand. We didn't see him again, and the 'party' cooled off immediately. Dylan went and helped himself to the fruit basket, and chatted 'Dude-talk' in the kitchen for a while. What had happened, he discovered, was that Bryan Dude had casually invited Brad and Pete back for drinks, and Brad and Pete had drunkenly over-interpreted the suggestion. All told, the Dudes had been pretty hospitable.

It was pretty obviously time to go. Frank wanted to apologise for all the noise we'd made so we decided to write a quick note and leave it on the coffee table. Dylan was the only one of us sober enough to hold a pen, but that didn't stop Frank from wanting his say.

'Sorry about the noise...' Dylan began, before the pencil and paper were eagerly snatched away from him. In the end, the note read:

'Sorry about the noise... bUt PeTE was FuCKeD.'

In fact Pete had so well disguised how fucked the rest of us were, that we didn't even really notice it until we left the house, and Frank instinctively tried to steal the Dudes' wheelie bin.

'No Frank,' we tried to explain. 'We were just at their house. They'll know it was us.'

'They won't!' he argued, moments before Bryan Dude opened the door and told us to bring their fucking bin back.

Beasting

Spring, and the early weeks of second semester, mark the official Beasting Season in St. Andrews. It's a time when old relationships are broken or renewed, and when fresh couplings can occur at a rate of several per week.

In celebration of this festive time, I bought a leg of Beast. This was thanks to Tesco's move to shift otherwise unwanted Turkey legs for 99p a shot. I could immediately see the possibilities ahead.

At a uniform price, it seemed like only good sense to go for quantity, and so I selected a drumstick of such awesome magnitude that it might rather have been used as a siege weapon, and dragged it home caveman style.

'It is the Beast,' I informed Frank, presenting it with a flourish. He needed no more convincing. Making a few hasty calculations, we were able to deduce that

1. The Beast Leg must, at one time, have belonged to a bird that meant business, and
2. The Beast Leg would take at least a fortnight to cook, plus marinade time.

'Better put the oven on, mate,' I said.

Luckily there were some primitive cooking instructions printed on the back of the styrofoam pack which rounded that figure down to somewhere pleasantly more in the region of two hours, so we prepared an oven tray and greased it up.

'I'm going to Fred Flintstone that badboy,' Frank said, cheerily.

We grabbed a few beers, and I tooled up an episode of Futurama or two. The air of anticipation was tangible. There may well have been some smoking, which would help to explain that tangible air, and also what happened next – if by 'next' you take me to mean 'two hours later, when Frank went down to the kitchen'.

The howls of rage and anguish were heard the length and breadth of the house. I thought at first that Frank must have poured boiling turkey fat over himself, perhaps as a result of some further Dude greeting. I wondered if maybe he had even collapsed under the sheer weight of the Beast, and was struggling to free his mangled legs from the wreckage. For all the commotion, it would have been as easy to imagine that the rest of the turkey had come back for revenge.

What had happened, in fact, was merely what had not happened; Frank had not, at any time, put the Beast into the oven. He was sitting crumpled in a chair, whimpering quietly to himself by the time I got down to the kitchen, his rage entirely replaced by impotent resignation.

'That's a new one on me, mate,' I informed him. 'I mean, not turning the oven on, fair enough. We've all been there. But... this?'

'It's raw,' he said, poking at the Beast as if willpower alone would be sufficient to cook a drumstick the size of Bristol. 'Fucking hell, Quinine.'

'I wondered what that mighty piece of chicken was doing out of the fridge,' Gowan said. 'Just sitting on the side like that.' We held Frank back.

'It's turkey,' Dylan said.

'It is the Beast,' I told them, authoritatively.

Brad

Brad was the first of us to embrace the seasonal Beast. He obviously fancied himself as something of a player, and plunged into the Dude movement with both feet, spending an inordinate amount of time with a spunky Dudette called Sallie. She had a boyfriend back in the states, but they were 'seeing other people'; almost all of them, in the analysis. It took a while for Brad to charm her, but I was rooting for him in a vaguely disapproving sort of a way.

I inadvertently helped out one night by inviting them both back to Fife Park for a nightcap, thereby providing them with an acceptably flimsy pretext to engage in intercourse. There were three of us in Brad's room, which was undeniably a crowd.

Taking secret pleasure in the thought that it had once been Craig's meticulously clean surface, I rolled a fat badboy and put my feet up. I outstayed my welcome somewhat by actually wanting to smoke the thing.

Brad took about three tokes and Sallie pretended to pass out, so I took the hint and left. I took my spliff with me. Frank and the randoms were asleep, so I played videogames for a while. Brad and Sallie were definitely, noisily awake for the next few hours.

Dylan and Frank came in to my room and complained, first thing next morning. They were both tired and grumpy. In some way, apparently, Brad's insatiable penchant for fucking was all my fault.

I'd actually been less disturbed than they had, which is to say that I had managed to fall asleep to the vibrant tune of two horny Yanks pumping, and not that it didn't deeply upset me in the psychological sense. That they were still at it when I got up in the middle of the night for a pee was the truly disturbing thing.

'It must've been all those cow hormones,' I said, as Frank stuck 'Mustang Sally' on at full volume.

'That'll teach them,' he said.

'How are you and Sallie?' someone asked Brad, later that week.

'Oh, you know,' he said. 'It's a girl thing, you know.'

We got Dylan to translate. He took it to mean 'not good'.

True to form, Brad was on some other girl's case by the end of the week, and Sallie seemed to have taken it upon herself to 'see' as many people as possible, within the narrow confines of her lifetime.

Gowan.

Gowan has a certain charm, you've got to give him that. He's got a bad history of one night stands on his record, including the Raisin Sunday affair in first year where he broke a ping pong table on which he was somewhat athletically screwing his academic sister. Poor Gowan never saw a deposit back in four straight years at St. Andrews.

After one of the early spring balls, Gowan satisfied an age-old desire of his which was, apparently, to make it with an Asian girl. On hearing this news, Mart very frankly declared that he didn't find Asian girls attractive, and I struggled to decide whether it was more racially prejudiced to maintain a blanket dislike of Asian women or go out with the express intention of screwing one.

The case in question was moot because Gowan did not succeed in hooking up with a particularly attractive Asian girl, which is a choice that translates well across most cultural barriers. He spent some time making out with her in Fife Park, and then escorted her home.

'I've always wanted to pull a hot Asian,' Gowan said, poking his head into the kitchen and giving us the thumbs up. I bit down the urge to wish him better luck next time. Dylan and I watched them leave, through the kitchen window.

'It takes all sorts,' I said, eventually.

'Yeah, and so does Gowan,' Dylan replied.

Will

Will's unstable girlfriend dumped him early in the year, which distinguished him as the only person in the house to have been given the heave by a certified mental. He didn't make any fewer trips back home afterwards, which really showed that he was in it for the horses.

Will's big night came at the Fencing Club dinner. Fencing was a big thing in Fife Park 7. Gowan and Will had joined at the start of the year and displayed an immediate proficiency with the foil, or at least an immediate passion for hurting each other with anything shaped vaguely like one. The competition between them bred a special kind of aggression, which could only be satisfied by a hole left in something or someone.

They used to face off along the downstairs corridor whenever they were drunk, fighting with whatever offensive weapons they could lay their hands on. In fact, as we later discovered, that's what had happened to the doors of rooms two and three, even before Frank got involved.

The dinner was an annual event for the Fencing Club, and books could probably be written solely about that. In fact, on the strength of a couple of the stories, combined of course with my longstanding desire to be a Jedi Knight[*], I joined the Fencing Club myself – too late though, for the club dinner that year, at which Will went for a thoroughly ambitious rebound fling.

He got very, very drunk, found two ladies of remarkable girth and, unable to choose between them, chose rather to take both girls home and divvy up whatever was left of his libido at the end of a hard night's drinking. It was, apparently, not very much. Both girls left heartily unsatisfied with proceedings, and Will passed out shortly afterwards.

The next day, Gowan stencilled the word *'some'* after the large 3 on Will's door. It was okay, because we all knew that the door was going to need replaced by that point.

Funnily enough, after hooching up on White Lightning that night, we caught a taxi into town whose driver was unable to resist telling us about his largest ever fare.

'My axle was creaking, I swear,' he said of the three costumed fornicators who had lately occupied his vehicle. 'A real skinny guy in the middle, but mind there wasn't a spare inch on the seat. All dressed like schoolgirls, they were.'

---

[*] Most people, even people in the club, don't realise that there's actually a genuine, directly traceable Kevin Bacon style connection between St. Andrews University Fencing Club and Darth fucking Vader.

135

Frank

I don't think Frank got any action. A girl came up to him in the bop one night, and seductively took his cigarette. She breathed smoke back at him with provocatively pursed lips.

'Fuck Off,' Frank said.

'Dude,' I told him.

'Bitch was after my smokes,' Frank said.

Dylan

Dylan is a strange one. He simultaneously knows what he wants, and is very shy. He sometimes speaks about sex, but with a kind of near-Buddhist reverence and a sage detachment that makes you wonder if he might not be confusing it with biblical exegesis. He has old-fashioned morals, or maybe he's ahead of his time and they're actually post-modern. I don't know quite what they are. There's a bit of guilt in there for sure, so they might be traditional after all. He shies away from vulgarity. He has an almost eastern respect for the body. He is quiet and reserved and will immediately turn his nose up at any particularly candid information with a hearty 'that's *awful*'.

That's one of the reasons I like to subject Dylan to whatever particularly sordid thing that comes to mind. The other is that he's one of those rare, few people who won't really think any less of you afterwards. I like to be honest with Dylan. As long as you can put up with being told that whatever else it may be it's also awful, then you're in the clear with him. I like that.

Dylan has a strange way with women, who will fall into his arms at a moment's notice, usually in a manner that hinders but does not preclude romance. In second year he met a girl called

Joanne, who was obviously the spawn of Highlanders and hippies. She was from so far up North that English might have been her second language.

There was a long lull period before they actually hit it off, although the point of no return probably came not too far into the semester.

However, Dylan did not Beast Joanne. Certainly he didn't Beast her at this stage, and then he didn't Beast her later either, because Dylan was above Beasting anyone.

Darcy and Euan

It was quite obvious that Darcy and Euan were going to hook up or flirt each other to death. I was completely unsurprised by the news that it had happened.

'I just can't believe it,' Darcy enthused.

'You've been talking about him for weeks,' I said.

'Yeah, but it was amazing.'

'Which part of the obvious, natural, and inevitable was the most shocking to you?' I asked.

'Alright, no need to get all bitchy,' Darcy said. 'I'm just sharing the news.'

'No, it's fine. Enjoy the moment,' I told her. 'I'm happy for you.'

The truth was that I was really pleased that two of my good friends had got together. I just wished it was two of my other friends, because, even though I didn't find Darcy that appealing, I was kind of in love with her. At least I think that I was, because it felt like my guts were in a vice every time I heard Euan's name.

This was no irrational, hopeless crush; I didn't even fancy Darcy. This was a different feeling, altogether. I kept an option on the hopeless part, though.

David Russell Apartments

There's no doubt I've put these pivotal moments of my life on unnecessary and undeserving pedestals. This book ought to be testament enough to that. But, apparently, I hold an undeserved reverence for the streets and buildings as well.

A few years ago, on discovering my old haunt David Russell Hall had been reduced to raw masonry, I found myself looking with a kind of venom at the newer and − let's be honest − much, *much* nicer David Russell Apartments.

Maybe it was that bracing Fife wind roiling over the plain, or maybe somebody had just told me what it was going to cost to stay in DRA for 38 weeks, but as I stood staring over the decimated landscape, I had to dab at my eyes.

Don't get me wrong, DRH was an abomination of a hall, and deserved to be razed to the ground by any civilized society. In the worst halls sweepstakes it was second only to the dark canker that is Andrew Melville, an atrocity of such magnitude that the earth itself has been attempting to swallow it since the mid eighties.

But DRH had *character*. It had *spirit*. It had *community*. All of which is a kind way of saying how naff the place was. It had those things by neglect as much as design but, sure, it had them. That was what let students make it their own. It was just run down enough to be open territory.

It had the same rules as the other halls, but they were out of place in a dive like DRH. The 'no blutack' rule seemed laughable in a place where the paint came off the walls if you coughed too hard. You used blutack anyway, and considered the warden lucky if you'd run out of permanent markers. That was what made those places a community; we were in it together, sure, but because we could own it, not just sleep in it.

You can't say that about the new halls. They've got an ethos. The people who made them still think about them, they're still proud of them. They can't be owned by students, because someone else has a claim. Those halls have still got a statement to make, an image to maintain. And fuck me, they've got a price tag to go with it. I stayed in Fife Park because I was poor, not because I liked sleeping on horsehair. Anyone willing to join me in that was part of the goddamn cause. Sometimes I wonder if it would have been more odd *not* to end up punching holes in the place.

Thinking about Fife Park again as a place, not just a set of memories, makes me want to go back. While it's still there. To do *something*. To remember it, or say goodbye, or take a picture. I don't know; it doesn't matter. I have nothing to give back to Fife Park, nothing to take from it. I've been writing about Fife Park for weeks, and I don't even know what I had there a decade ago. This is the nature of nostalgia. Not just a longing for something long past, but a longing disconnected from tangible wants, and hardwired straight to desire itself, for its own sake, with no outlet.

Whatever I'm looking for, I won't find it in brickwork. Besides, most of Fife Park seems to have been made from cardboard.

David Russell Hall

Craig called me up one night, at about three in the morning, to tell me that he had taken some strange pills and was probably going to die. He was remarkably cheerful about it. I thought he was drunk.

'Where did you get the pills?' I asked him.

'Some guy's cupboard,' he told me. 'I had two! I mean, I don't know what those things were. They could be for anything.'

'What did they look like?' I asked him.

'I don't know,' he said. 'Like pieces of chalk. For all I know you're supposed to clean the toilet with them.'

'Well, who did you get them from?'

'Nobody, we just found them.'

'You just found some toilet cleaning pills, so you thought you'd pop a couple?'

'Yeah, man, pretty much. Oh, God, Sandy's passed out. I think he's stopped breathing....' He paused. 'No. wait. He's okay.' I could hear Sandy giggling in the background at this point.

'Where did you find them?'

'The pills? In some cupboard in the bathroom. I'm feeling pretty sleepy now, man.'

'Which bathroom? Whose cupboard? Craig?'

'Sandy took a light. You know, one of those UV ones?'

'What about the pills? Did he take them, too?'

'Yeah, well, he took half of one. He's a pussy. He was going to take both halves but he chickened out on me.'

'Whose idea was it to take them in the first place?'

That was a stupid question. Sandy and Craig didn't have ideas, they just escalated each other into madness. When they lived together in fourth year, they stole a garden, right down to the last gnome.

'Well, I'm going to bed now. Night, Quinn.'

'Are you okay, Craig?'

'Yeah, yeah, I'm probably going to die.'

'Right. Sleep well.'

'Chuh. Okay, well, look, goodbye.'

'Right.'

Of course, I threw on some clothes and prepared to dash around there right away.

'Frank,' I shouted. 'Frank!'

Frank showed up in his boxer shorts.

'Did you break my fucking record?'

'Frank,' I said, 'it's Craig. He's taken some crazy pills.'

'Another mystery solved,' Frank said.

'Seriously, I think he's poisoned himself.'

'How many did he take?' Frank said.

'Two,' I said. 'He found them in some cupboard at a party.'

'Yeah, I wouldn't worry about it.'

'They could be fucking anything, he says.'

'Two of anything won't kill you,' Frank said. He turned to leave.

'Aren't you fucking coming?' I asked.

'My work here is done.'

'You can't be so fucking sure,' I said, churning with frustration.

'No,' Frank said. He shrugged.

'He's a mate,' I said. 'He's a mate.'

'And one of the many advantages of a medical background is not needing to give a shit when your mates go rooting through the medicine cabinet.'

'I'm fucking going anyway,' I said.

'I know.'

'Seriously, Frank. What do I fucking do?'

'Chill out,' he said. 'Maybe take one of those pills.'

I ran across the Fife Park car park in a dirty T-shirt, with no socks on under my trainers.

The block door was ajar, so I pelted right up to Craig's landing. I literally stumbled on Sandy, as I got there. He lay, curled in a foetal position, cradling a metre long strip light.

'Are you okay Sandy?' I asked. He was shivering. His forehead was beaded with sweat.

'New level!' he said. 'New level.'

Craig's door was open, and he was on his bed, staring up at the ceiling.

'Craig,' I said.

I stood in the doorway, not wanting to enter without an invitation, despite myself.

'Hey Quinn,' Craig said. 'What's up?'

'You called,' I said.

'Mm.'

'You took some pills.'

'And a blacklight.'

'How are you feeling?'

'He just unplugged it and put it on the windowsill,' Craig said.

'The light?'

'Yeah. We were at a party.'

'Where?'

'I don't know, do I? Oh, God, it was yahed-up to the max.'

'You got the pills at the party?'

It was detective work. Craig was evidently fucked out of his face, and Sandy was dribbling on the carpet.

'Everyone was watching him like he'd gone crazy. But he just walked out of the room calm as a breeze. Then when we got outside he grabbed it from the other side, and ran like hell.'

'The pills, though.'

'Yeah, we stole those too. From the bathroom cupboard!'

'Okay. That makes sense. Can I see the pills? Are there any left?'

'Sandy's got them.'

He did. He was clutching about five or six of them in one sweaty palm.

They looked like horse pills. There was no way that they were intended for human consumption, and you'd have to have been a fool to think so. I laughed despite myself.

'Well, you're in unfamiliar territory here,' I said.

They were oval shaped, and had little green speckles in them. They did seem to be made of chalk.

It's possible you were meant to dissolve them in something. It's also possible that you were meant to clean toilets with them. They didn't smell of anything. I half expected them to smell like herbal extract, or bath salts. If they had been scented lavender, then everything would have fallen into place. My mind was running over what I should do. I couldn't think of a thing that made sense.

I took a deep breath. I wasn't going to do anything. Not this time.

I wasn't going to run around being the one who was worried all the time. Fucking Craig wasn't even worried, and he had two toilet pills in his gut. Frank wasn't worried. Sandy wasn't... Well, Sandy was licking a stolen blacklight, I wasn't about to take his views into account. The only person who was worried was me. I don't even know why Craig called me. Maybe he just figured *someone* should be worried, and he thought of me first.

I wasn't going to be that guy. No fucking way was I going to be the person everyone thought of as the worrier. And, I guess it was just coincidence, but I was finding it increasingly harder to be worried as new information emerged.

Maybe a bit of Frank was rubbing off on me after all, but it just seemed so unlikely that anything bad would happen. You can't swallow a comedy sized pill and die, I thought. That just doesn't make sense. That would be like choking to death on a clown nose.

'I think that you're probably going to die,' I said to Craig. The words felt light on my tongue.

It was a curious mix of possible and improbable. It was funny. Craig thought so, too.

'So I'm going home,' I said. 'Nothing to do, here.'

'Well, night mate,' he replied.

'You going to shut the door?' I asked.

'No, no. I think I might just leave it.'

'Right.'

'New level,' Sandy added.

'Well, then. I think I'm going back to bed.'

'Right.'

'Bye,' I said.

The next day, shopping for peaches and toothpaste in Tesco, I caught sight of a shelf full of bubble bath. I don't know why I was drawn to it. There weren't any baths in Fife Park. I couldn't get it out of my head. It was on special, I guess. Later on in the day, I turned up on the DRH landing with a bottle of bubble bath and a towel.

Craig was fine. Sandy was stressing about something, which was as fine as he was going to get in essay season. I went and had a nice long soak. We never figured out what the pills were, but I suppose it doesn't matter.

Smoking Gun

When I was in Fife Park, smoking wasn't the big social taboo that it is these days. Some people smoked and some people didn't, and those that did were just smart people doing a dumb thing. A lot has changed in a decade. I heard some five year old ask 'Mummy, why is that man smoking?' on the street a few weeks ago. And she replied 'Because he's a bad man.'

The bad man was me, on another weeklong lapse in my commitment to not smoking. It started with that one fucking joint I smoked. Seems like nothing comes without a price these days.

'I am *not* a bad man,' I said to the kid.

Not that I really know if that's true, but I'll be damned if a cigarette's going to inculpate me. There was an awkward pause.

'Well, I'm not,' I told the parent, who was looking at me like I was a rapist offering her gardening tips.

'You wouldn't understand,' she said. 'You're not a mother.'

'Well shit, you're not a smoker,' I told her, which was the exact point at which I realised that I was going to have to go through the hassle of quitting again.

'Ah, fuck it,' I said.

'Fuck!' the kid said. 'Fuck it, bad man!'

The kid was right. I have studied the art of quitting smoking for years, and I can tell you that 'Fuck it' justifies anything and stands for nothing. Fuck it, you say, and light another.

I remember one time I asked Frank what it felt like to need a smoke, long before I ever touched a deck of fags.

'It feels like you need a cigarette,' he said.

'But is it like hungry?' I pressed. 'Or more like thirsty?' He considered it for long enough to give a reasoned answer.

'It just feels like you need a cigarette,' he said. He lit up.

It didn't sound so bad, and I let it creep up on me. It's all meaningless until you're there, of course. Most things are. For me, it is a little like thirst; maybe I put the idea into my own damn head. Whatever, it's only there when you're feeling the physical withdrawal, right when you'd be about to have another. That passes in days; a thirst of no consequence. Then, well done, you've quit.

But it doesn't feel like thirst when you want one after that. When you want one every day – weeks after, months after, even years after, because sometimes it feels like it was all you ever really looked forwards to doing. Then it feels like a raw bitch.

Sure, you sometimes forget about cigarettes when you've stopped smoking them, but only till you remember. That's when you get taken by surprise, and then you're halfway to the filter before you realise what you're holding.

I always quit again. It's not the fear of cancer. You can take that for granted, and it doesn't mean a thing. You get the odd panic attack or hurts-to-breathe scare, and then you get right back to it. Hardly any smokers can connect with the smoker's death, not directly. It's not the thought of dying that makes me quit.

It's the embarrassment. The shame of it. The shame in my head when I imagine telling the people I love that I am sick or dying because a small pleasure was more important to me than everything else I'm worth.

That works. I can't easily see my death, but that I can see. That dark vignette is somehow too *real* to be my future, and then I think, *how much more real is actually dying, than merely being in awe of it?* That's the break point. Then the whole dark, sticky, spewing end is made real through other eyes than mine, and in that reflection I can stare down the gorgon. And I don't want it.

This unhardy sense of mortality is new, and not new. When I was 20 years old I was unlived in as a person. Every cigarette or joint was as safe as the first, which was safe enough for a while. But I had my eye on the future, even then. I was afraid of the things unlike myself that I might become, and maybe did, which is a kind of death.

Well, I don't want to be the same person I was then, any more than he wanted to be me. But I want to feel his passion, his willing, his daily excitement. And I would like one concrete thing I can point at, and tell him why he was wrong to be afraid.

The Wood and The Burn

The hallway of Fife Park Seven was littered with drinking trophies. There were road signs, bar signs, poles and sticks, and one night Frank even brought back a full rotary clothes line, which he erected over my bed, while I was sleeping. Then he pegged an old pair of pants above my nose.

Frank was not a discriminating poacher. While Gowan and Will were the steeliest of scavengers, with a discerning eye for genuinely ambitious trophies, Frank would simply uproot whatever was largest and nearest to him on the way home, and leave it somewhere funny or inconvenient.

Because I was, according to various reports, 'weak sauce' or 'a total pussy', I did not bring home trophies. I have a personal rule about not stealing [*]. I guess I must have been missing out on the thrill of dragging some weighty object home, and the resulting satisfaction of the age old hunter-gatherer instinct, because one night, I broke my rule – and possibly some others, too.

Frank and I had been drinking together in the Tudor, avoiding local trouble as best we could, but we got out of there before closing time. I suggested that we take two gigantic wooden constructions that were leaning against a skip on Greyfriars.

'Nobody wants them,' Frank said, but that was beside the point, and false in any case, since *I* wanted them.

So Frank acquiesced, if nothing else because of their sheer size. That was his style, at least. They were at least eight or nine feet

---

[*] I'm so averse to the idea of stealing, that I've even been known to *unsteal*, by making copies of things like movies, games, music...

long, and looked like different sides of the same construction project. They looked like rafters, or the blades of some gigantic wooden sled, but they were made of a fairly light wood, and we could easily manage one each.

'Want to go home a well wicked way?' Frank asked.

'Maybe?' I said, wondering if it would involve anybody's garden.

'Down by the KFB,' he told me. 'There's like this secret path. I went home that way last night. It was well scary.'

'OK,' I said. 'Can we take the wood?'

'Yes, Quinine,' Frank conceded. 'It's a crazy way, though. I was well freaked out walking back last night. It's really dark.'

'Right,' I said. 'Enough, mate. You sold me on it already.'

I figured that I was holding an eight foot piece of timber, which certainly put me in the ballpark of formidable. Frank was equally well equipped, and furthermore, he was apparently also the Walrus. It seemed obvious that if there were to be a meeting of two parties on this secret way, then I had probably picked the best side.

The 'secret way' turned out to be a wide and well trodden footpath, running alongside the Kinnessburn. It was neither dark nor foreboding, but did provide enough space for Frank to swing his wood at more or less arm's length. He did just that for a few minutes, until it began to tire him. Then, standing at the edge of the path, he raised the artefact above his head with both hands, and announced 'I am the wood!'

Unfortunately, on this particular occasion, Frank was not the wood. Nor was he in any way at one with the wood, or even

151

particularly aware of how the wood was getting on. It was overbalancing him, in fact, so that he had to take a small step backwards to counter the effect.

Behind Frank there was a slope. He had to take a slightly larger step backwards to counter its influence on his centre of gravity. The slope did not stop after that step, and neither did Frank. He continued to fight for his balance, seemingly in slow motion, until he reached the bottom of the slope, at a pace I've never seen him approach before or since.

Behind the slope was a ten foot drop, at the bottom of which lay only the Kinnessburn and some sharp rocks, and not necessarily in that order. Frank did a backwards roll into the void, sending his wooden Waterloo spinning into the air alongside him. There was a sickening crunch as Frank landed on the rocks, and another slightly less sickening 'whump' as the wood landed on Frank. Then there was silence.

I ran to the top of the slope without pausing for thought, to find Frank floating face down in the burn.

'Frank,' I shouted. 'Fuckmefuckmefuckme. Frank!'

Scrambling down the slope on my butt cheeks, I reached the drop in a matter of seconds. I struggled to let myself down to the burn, trying as best I could to keep the human casualties down to one.

'Fuck,' Frank said, standing up.

'Fucking hell, Frank,' I said, 'I thought you were dead. Are you alright?'

He didn't reply. He just turned his head from side to side, scanning the scenery and looking for all the world as if he had woken up on Mars. He waded into the middle of the burn and looked around, before patting his pockets down. He found what he was looking for in his shirt.

'Thank fuck,' he said, reaching into the deck. 'My cigarettes are dry. I really fucking need a cigarette.'

I sat on the bank, while Frank stood in the burn, murky water flowing around his knees. He stood there for minutes on end, finished his smoke before he made any effort to move. He looked strangely thoughtful.

'Let's go home,' he said. 'I'm fucking soaked.'

'Are you hurt?' I asked him. 'Are you concussed?' There was blood in his hair.

'Dunno,' he said, climbing out of the water. I grabbed the wood and followed him.

Frank's secret way narrowed until it ran through what looked like somebody's garden gate and, from there, went on to Lade Braes. We walked along the path as it goes parallel to Hepburn Gardens and along the top side of Cockshaugh Park, and eventually came out a short traipse from Fife Park.

We dropped the wood in the hallway, and went into the kitchen. Dylan was making something with cheese, so we recounted the story for him, and then again when Gowan came in.

Frank, standing in the burn, knee deep in running water, blood dripping from his matted hair, smoking a cigarette like nothing could have hurt him; that's the moment I remember from that year. That's what I wanted to be, what I sometimes felt I was. Defiant, vigorous, and immortal.

'He's still bleeding,' Gowan said.

'Tell Will the bit about the backflip,' Dylan said.

As I talked it up, Frank interrupted every so often, swearing that there had been an old style bathtub in the burn, and that he had thought for just one moment that he could climb into it and sail off down the stream.

There might have been, I'll say that much, but I certainly never saw one.

The Tortoise and the Hare

I mostly pretend my life began when I got to St. Andrews. It takes the edge off being thirty and it's easy to believe, because I hardly did a thing until I was twenty. I never knew what I was missing.

I hung with the wrong crowd at school and not in the cool way, where everyone smokes behind the bike sheds, but in the uncool way where you're a geek with no social skills and most of your friends are into collectible card games or masturbation. It was a time of insecurity, panic and confusion.

I hated every fucking minute of it. I spent a lot of time in the school library. I went right home at the end of the day, kept my head down all the way. I played video games and read books all night. I only kept in with a few friends after it was all finished up, and I thought the place and every memory of it could burn. I was, essentially, a non person for two decades. I missed out on every good story the kids used to tell about those days.

I never felt anyone up on a pile of coats. I never made a crowd cheer. I never danced without a care. I never danced and made anyone else care. I never started conversations. I never got laid, never went out with girls, never dressed up, or got wild. I never let my hair down. I never grew it long. I never calibrated against the social scale.

And, even when I got to St. Andrews, I still didn't know what I was missing; but I knew it was late in the day to be missing it. Something Darcy said brought all of this back to me.

'You're going fucking *bald*!'

She pronounced the word 'bald' as if it might have been of interchangeable credulity with 'Clive, the incredible death-defying mongoose'.

'Thanks, Darcy,' I said. 'It's your sensitivity that I appreciate most.'

'Seriously,' she said. 'There's a patch as big as my fist with, like, no hair at all.'

I know, it doesn't seem like much.

But it made me realise that I was at the end of being a teenager, and I still hadn't done a single thing that teenagers are good for, except maybe sleeping too much and whining about the pain of being alive. There was clearly a world of shit to catch up on, some of which was always going to be a stretch, and some of which could be as easy as a trip to Superdrug.

I showed up at Darcy's place around six, with a bottle of vodka, two litres of orange juice, and a pack of Garnett Red hair dye, with primer.

'You busy?' I asked.

'I'm not ready,' she said. 'You're about two hours early.'

She tapped her wrist, as if this was so fucked up that it might be her watch that was out.

'Yeah,' I said. 'But I had an idea.'

'Does it involve me not getting ready? Because no go, sunshine. I'm not hanging out with your flatmates looking like a drag queen.'

I started unpacking the carrier bags onto her kitchen work surface.

'It involves *me* getting ready. And you look fine.'

'You could have got the decent vodka,' she said.

'It was an extra six quid. Have you got any other mixers in?'

'Coke? So... what's going on?'

I produced the hair dye with a flourish.

'I have no idea how this works,' I said. 'But I'm pretty sure you've done it before.'

'Seriously?' she said.

'How long does it take?'

'Couple of hours? No, less. You've got less hair.'

'Fuck's sake,' I said.

'I mean it's shorter. God, you're touchy. If you're that sensitive, I don't think Nuclear Orange is going to be your thing.'

'It's Garnett,' I said. 'And anyway, I can shave it all off right after if I don't like it. It's not like I won't have to do that soon enough anyway.'

'It's your bag, hun,' she said, taking the box off me, and browsing the label. 'You bought good stuff, at least.'

'Alright,' I said. 'So how do we do this?'

'Start by pouring two of those.'

I guess it goes without saying, but she was pointing at the vodka.

The peroxide smell burned the back of my nose something chronic. I couldn't stand it in Darcy's tiny bedroom. I had to walk out onto the landing and waft away from my head with the old towel that Darcy had supplied.

'Fucking stinks,' I said. 'Stings, too.'

'It does, a bit,' she said. 'We should have done a test patch on your skin first, to make sure you aren't allergic.'

'But we didn't,' I said.

'No time,' she said. 'You'll be fine. Just say if it really burns.'

'Only my eyes.'

'Probably fumes, if it's just making you want to blink. Don't rub them, for fuck's sake.'

We left the red stuff in for forty eight minutes, even though the instructions said no more than twenty five. The first forty minutes were planned, and the rest was because we were onto the fourth vodka orange, and arguing about how orange juice was made.

'They make it back up with water,' I said. 'I swear.'

'There's no point,' she said. 'That would be like mixing... cream with water to get, like, ordinary milk.'

'That's why it says *made from concentrate*,' I said. 'Did you reckon they were just thinking about oranges really hard while they did it?'

'Don't be a fucking smartass,' she said. 'What, you going to go on mastermind, with fucking.... juice... as your specialist subject?'

She hiccupped, hard.

We went into the bathroom and I knelt at the bathtub while Darcy held the showerhead and massaged all the lather and goop out and down the drain. I felt my heart beat hard in time with Darcy's rhythmic scrubbing, felt my pulse banging against the side of my straining neck.

We put the industrial strength conditioner in, and the hair began to feel a bit less like frayed electrical wire. I admired myself in the steamy mirror.

'We've created a monster,' Darcy said, stumbling on her feet.

'I'm still me,' I said.

But I didn't feel like me, any more. I felt like someone who had done something, even if it was something as simple as changing the colour of my hair. I felt this self-aware smile tugging at my face, and it wasn't my smile, either. It was thinner, and more assured.

'I'm an idiot,' I said.

'But you had to let the world know.'

'Hell, yes.'

'Vodka's gone. Gimme five minutes to change.'

When she called me back into the bedroom, she wasn't properly dressed.

'Sit down,' she said. I did.

'What's up? You're not done.'

'You,' she said. 'You're such my best friend.'

'Sweet,' I said. 'You're wasted.'

'No,' she said. Then more firmly. 'No! Look at me.'

I looked back at her. Right into her eyes. Saw them focus at a half speed.

'You know I've been dealing with a lot of stuff,' she said. 'And you're always there, and I need that, and I'm really happy for that.'

'It's OK,' I said. 'You're a friend.'

'You make things alright,' she said. 'Come here.'

She leaned in and hugged me, squeezing my shoulders.

'I never talk to anyone, except you,' she said. 'It's important.'

'Everyone has things going on.'

'No,' she said. 'Not like really, really heavy things.'

She looked at me, meaningfully. I didn't get it. I only saw my own meanings. I stared into her eyes, and felt like I had all the time in the world. I didn't need to turn away, felt I could stare into those eyes until they couldn't stare back. I felt excitement, control, anticipation. Anticipation, yes, but with an acceptance, and readiness, that was all new.

'What?' she said.

But I didn't answer. There was no need. We held our eyes in a lock, so that the world fell away at the edges, leaving only a tunnel of light between us. Darcy leaned forwards, put her arms around me again. Her lips brushed at the corners of mine. I turned my head by the smallest fraction, and then we were kissing. I ran my hands up her side, and she grabbed my head. She pulled me down to the bed, closed her eyes.

Then she was unconscious.

'Oh, for fuck's sake,' I said.

I lay down next to her, stared at the ceiling.

'Well,' I said. 'We've got all the time in the world, now.'

VolcanoHead

Time makes fools of us all. By break of morning things were a mess. I was wretched hung over with a crick in my back and Darcy had gone to the bathroom in situ. She didn't remember the kiss. I sat with my head pulsing in my palms while she cleaned herself up. The hope drained out of it all. When I told her, she couldn't bear the thought of it.

'How could you?' she said.

'Because I wanted to,' I told her. 'I thought you wanted to, as well.'

'Don't be stupid,' she said.

'Well I'm sorry for thinking it took two people to kiss,' I said.

'I was drunk.'

'When are you not?' I asked. 'And I'm always drunk with you, it's all we ever do.'

'I trusted you,' she said.

'And *you kissed me*,' I told her. 'It was a bigger deal for me, right?'

'No,' she said, sadly. 'Because I *only* trusted you.'

We worked it out, as best we could, but we were tired and sick. Eventually we said it was OK between us, but knew it wasn't.

I walked back to Fife Park in the dawn light. Sky was all blue and grey. I grabbed my guitar, went out and sat on our garden path, my ass resting up against the doorstep. It was a curious mix of warm and deepest cold. I cut a pose against the breeze, found a chord on the neck of my Strat, put it all out of my mind. Fife

Park was the place to be, and I was on holiday from everywhere else.

The G string snapped, with the first strum. It rasped across the other strings, and a sharp end of it flicked me in the face, just below my eye. The stinging pain enraged me. The broken string was maddening. Just when I had it all together. Fucking, just when I had it all together.

I grabbed the neck of the guitar, and brought the body down hard on the flagstones. The body held, but the veneer fractured. It was chipboard, underneath. I leapt to my feet, and swung again.

'Fuck you!' I screamed. 'Fuck you! Fuck you! Fuck you!'

I brought it down over and over again, at different angles, until cracks ran over the entire frame of the guitar, but it still held.

'Fuck you,' I said at last, and threw the guitar over my shoulder. It bounced off the wall of Fife Park 8, and landed in the bushes near the front door. I walked away. I just walked.

Fussball

First time I'd been out on the town in a couple of weeks, and I felt like shit. Darcy had asked me not to tell a soul. I was a bit lost, but I held to that. There were a million things I needed to get off my chest. She'd asked me not to call, so I didn't. She told me she needed space, so I gave it. Somehow it was all about her, and that made me bitter.

I'd spent a couple of straight days in bed, sulking. I'd spent a couple of quiet weeks sitting in. Luckily it was essay season, so there was plenty to procrastinate over. But Frank kept inviting me out, and eventually I ran out of excuses. I was moping over a nasty pint for about an hour. Frank had little time for this.

'You're a miserable bastard,' he said.

'I've got things going on,' I said.

'Sure,' he said. 'But are they as important as my winning streak?'

'Winning streak?'

'Since you started being a whiny bitch and staying home, me and Paedo haven't lost a match of table football. Not even against South African Dude.'

South African Dude was a pure legend at the table, and also not even vaguely South African. He could trap a ball and put pressure on the paddles till the bars bent. Eventually the ball would shoot directly into the goal of its own volition, rather than suffer any more.

'I thought I was irreplaceable,' I said.

'Yeah, well. I've had to make do.'

'I'll get over it,' I said.

I rubbed my forehead with the tips of my fingers. Took another tiny sip from my warming pint.

'We could play the quiz?' Frank said.

'I'm not fussed,' I said.

Frank scowled. He wasn't about to make another concession.

'I know,' Frank said. 'About you and Darcy.'

That broke the tension. I felt my shoulders heave with a great winding rush of relief.

'Oh, thank fuck,' I gasped. I could have hugged him right there and then. 'How'd you find out?'

'From Euan, actually.'

'Fuck me, I didn't know she'd told him yet. How's he taking it?'

'He's really into his Shitokan Karate at the moment,' Frank told me. 'I'm sure that's helping him work it out of his system.'

'Shotokan, you mean.'

'Like that,' Frank said. 'But you learn to beat the shit out of people who mess with your woman.'

'Dude,' I said.

'Sorry, Quinn, but this is funny. You're properly reaping what you've sown here.'

Had to be that the extreme sport that Euan had thrown himself into this semester was some form of the art of ass-kicking.

'I feel lousy,' I said. 'About everything.'

'Welcome to it,' he said. 'Still looking for advice?'

'Mate, whatever you've got.'

'This is it,' he said. 'This is how it is, all the time, for everyone. You didn't fuck up, you just got promoted a division.'

'This is how it is for you, too?' I asked.

'Shit, no. I don't get involved,' Frank said. 'It looks messy.'

'See, I'd like to be like that,' I said.

'No,' Frank said. 'You want all kinds of things.'

'Yeah, ' I said. 'But I'd like to handle them like you do.'

'Well, I can understand that,' Frank said, swelling. 'Who wouldn't want to be like me? But you can't, because you've forgotten the most important thing.'

'Which is?'

'That I'm the Daddy,' Frank said. 'And you're not.'

Darcy Loch and the Last Midnight Walk

Darcy sent me an email. 'We've got to talk.' It was damn near three in the morning, but we were obviously both awake. I went over, post haste.

It had been a curious few weeks of half-pleasant exchanges. It's not like we didn't see each other, in fucking St. Andrews. But we didn't talk to each other – or quite ignore each other either.

'Hi,' she'd mumble, and move right on down the street.

'You OK?' I'd ask.

'Just need some space, some time,' she might say.

It was pregnant, like it always was with us. First one tension, then another.

This time we were expecting to finish something, and we'd be doing it at her leisure. She was well-prepared when I arrived: house was empty, throw was all tidy on the couch, couple of mugs of tea on the lounge table. It could have been a date, but it so obviously wasn't.

'It's been a rough few weeks,' she said, as if for both of us.

'Has it?' I asked. 'I'm sorry.'

I wanted out, but I stood my ground. She sat, so I sat. Opposite ends of the couch. Just like the tea on the table, come to think of it. I took mine, cradled it in my cold palms.

'I'm still really angry about what happened,' she said. 'But I realise that I was responsible, too.'

'Well,' I said, diplomatically. 'We were both there.'

'I think we need to get it out in the open,' she said. 'I'm ready now.'

'I don't mind talking,' I said. 'How's Euan taken it?'

'I told him,' she said.

'I know. It was the right thing.'

'He thought I was going to leave him.'

'No,' I said, looking at my feet.

'Of course not.'

'So what now?'

'I don't like things being like this, with us.'

'Awkwardness always fades,' I said. 'I should fucking know.'

'It is awkward,' she said.

'It won't last.'

'It won't be the same again, either.'

'No. You've always been right about that.'

'I've lost so many friends.'

'Yes.'

'I don't want us not to be friends.'

'What is this to you?' I asked.

'It's just...'

She broke, as if to cry.

'So, we'll be friends,' I said.

'Why did you kiss me?'

'I loved you.'

'Do you know for sure?'

'In the end. You must have known, too.'

'Well, I suppose I always wondered.'

She ran her hand up her arm, as if it were cold.

'I'm not expecting some grand happy ending,' I said.

'I just don't think of you like that,' she said.

'You did, though,' I said. 'It was your kiss, first.'

'That's not why.'

'Why then?' I asked.

'Because I trusted you.'

She crossed her legs, put her feet up onto the couch, grabbed one in each hand. She fidgeted with her toes. We sat there, quietly, taking in what meanings we could snatch from the cloud of our half sentences.

'How could a feeling like that be a bad thing?' I said, at last.

'It depends on who you are,' she told me.

'How *do* you think of me?' I asked her.

She shrugged, and took a sip of tea. Looked into the mug.

'You said *loved*,' she said.

'I think that kiss broke a kind of balance,' I told her.

'Yes.'

'We needed different things, from different directions.'

'We've passed each other by,' she said. 'It's over, maybe.'

'We're friends,' I said. 'We're going to be, still.'

'It's never going to mend completely,' she said.

'It's not really about being mended,' I told her.

Somewhere in it all was the truth that I didn't spot for years to come. I walked back to Fife Park as the horizon rolled over and turned blue again. The sky is so large in St. Andrews.

The East Nuke

We came back to the house to cap a night off, late some time in April. Mart was with me, Craig had declined as usual. Fife Park was dead to him, apparently.

Frank had been away with medics all night. We couldn't see in the kitchen as we came over the lawn; the windows were all steamed up. But there was movement. There were raised voices. One raised voice, anyway.

Mart ran upstairs to use the john, and I went to investigate. In the downstairs hall, one of the Randoms had his door half open and was peering round it. Kitchen door was shut, as were the other two rooms. If the other Randoms were home they weren't showing.

'Hey Dylan,' I said.

'I think Frank went crazy,' he said.

'Mmm.'

'He broke half of everything, I reckon.'

'You been in there?'

'Almost. Look, can you speak to him, before he breaks everything else?'

'I don't know what to say. Did you speak to him?'

'He wouldn't answer me.'

'I don't know what I can tell you,' I said.

'Just, he might listen to you.'

I stepped up. My hand reached out for the handle, but I couldn't bring myself to open the door.

'You fucking cunting bitching fuck.'

With each expletive, there was a bang. As if someone were hitting something in time with their own rage.

'You cunting fucking mothercunting shit fucker!'

'Who's he shouting at?' Mart asked, appearing behind me. 'What's going on?'

'Nothing,' I said. 'It is what it is.'

'Very Zen,' Mart said. 'You should get in there. He might hurt himself.'

I pushed the door open, and a spray of porcelain flew past my nose, right to left. It was *my* porcelain. Another mug hit the door before it was half open. I poked my head around the door.

'Hello,' I said.

Frank was standing over by the cooker, with half a plate in his hand.

'This fucking plate,' he said. He threw it at the floor, where it shattered, the fresh pieces mixing with the wreckage of half our crockery.

'And this mug,' he said.

He hefted it into the air almost gently, but quickly spun the golf club round to intercept it. I pulled my head back into the hallway just in time. I could hear tinkling pieces of it hitting the floor. I shut the door.

'Fucking bastarding shiteating cuntbreathing fucking cocksores.' Frank's voice was muffled, but still loud.

'Cocksores, huh?' Mart said.

'Are you alright in there?' I shouted through. No answer.

'Hello?' Mart called.

I looked in again. The cupboard doors were off, lying on top of a pile of broken bowls and plates. Frank rested his hands on the work surface for stability, and then kicked out at the drawers. It took one kick for each of them to lose their facades. Pots and pans spilled out onto the floor, and crunched onto broken porcelain.

Frank turned around, angry wildness in his eyes. He scanned the room, and found his golf club leaning up against the table. He grabbed it, grimaced for a moment, and then smacked it into the counter.

'OK, Frank,' I said. 'OK.'

I stepped out of the room, neatly, and shut the door for the last time. There was nothing in that room I cared about apart from Frank, and he was on his own path.

'We're going to let him work it out,' I said.

Mart nodded.

'Whatever it is. I don't care about the kitchen,' I said.

I never knew what drove Frank, and I never knew what he cared about. One night he went crazy with a golf club, and I still don't know why. I asked him about it later, but he was coy. He was embarrassed. God, that took the edge off things. The man who didn't give a fuck getting shy on me.

He didn't want me to talk about it, he didn't want it to be his story, didn't want it to be in this story; the night that Frank went nuts and trashed the place. I wouldn't even write it down, except that it is so much a part of *my* story. How much it changed my own perception of the place.

Once that happened, there was no way that things were how I thought they were. And though I've thought about it for years since, I still don't know how they were. It's just shit that happened.

'I reckon he caught his Dad cheating with another woman,' Craig said, later.

'He probably failed another year,' Mart said.

'Could be a girl thing,' Dylan said. 'I mean, we don't know.'

'I don't think we really know at all,' I said.

'You never really know people.'

'You could take someone apart piece by piece, and still never know them,' Craig said. He looked like he thought it might be a good side-project.

'Maybe that's Frank and Fife Park,' Mart said.

'I hope he found what he was looking for,' Dylan said. 'If not, I reckon it's probably in pieces by now.'

May Dip

We'd all done it in first year. I had been particularly drunk, and wound up on the beach more or less by accident, while looking for my door keys. At the time, I hadn't even heard of the May Dip, let alone brought a towel, but I was entering that subtle state of suggestibility that comes at the end of a long day and a lot of alcohol. Hell, I would have gone in fully clothed if Mart, who coincidentally had just the door keys I was looking for, hadn't advised me to strip at least to my boxers.

Considering myself a May Dip veteran, I thought that we would be off the hook in second year. I was dead wrong, as Frank mindfully insisted that we hadn't done it properly the first time, and would have to go again. Knowing Frank, I had an idea of what 'doing it properly' would entail.

'You mean in the buff, right?' I asked.

'Why stop short?'

'Because, at the top of a long list of reasons, other people will see my penis.'

'That's happened on all my best nights,' Frank said.

'Yeah, it's just not a good idea.'

'Medically, it's the running into the sea that I'd come down against,' Frank said. 'Nudity never hurt anyone. Well, probably some people who work with heavy machinery, or deep fat fryers or something.'

'Well, I'm not doing it,' I said. 'I mean, I'll do the dip again if I have to, but not with my bollocks on display.'

'I think you should,' Frank said.

'Yeah, well, I don't care.'

'Fine,' Frank said. 'But there's no point pretending to be all wild and free, and running into the sea waving your arms like you just don't care about anything, if you need a pretty little pair of frilly pink panties on to do it.'

'That sounds even more crazy,' I said.

'That was a bad example,' Frank said. 'But do whatever you want. Obviously, I just thought that you were the one who was all interested in pushing his limits and not giving a fuck and all that jazz. But that's fine.'

'I don't really see how this pushes...' I began.

'Also, can I just say that if you don't do it, you'll be bottling it. Properly,' Frank added.

Once I had agreed to it in principle, there was no going back.

The meat of the tradition known as the 'May Morning Dip' is short enough to relay in a single sentence: at the first break of dawn on May 1st, run screaming into the ocean from the beach of Castle Sands. All other worthy aspects of this insane annual observance can be summed up with a single corollary: immediately run out again, screaming, if possible, louder.

We decided to have a bit of a party leading up to the event, partly because any excuse for a few drinks was a good enough one, but mostly because we were all adamant that 4.37am should come firmly towards the end of a day, and never anywhere near the beginning of one. Also, when you're talking about running bollock naked into the North Sea in the glow of the breaking dawn, sobriety is the only real handicap.

The rendezvous was at Euan McWinslow's place in Gatty, where we were also celebrating the birthday of a guy called Dick, whose major party piece was leaping out of the upstairs window into a bed of roses next to the front door. It wasn't the best trick I'd ever seen, but it sure made people shit themselves when they rang the doorbell.

It wasn't the first time I'd hung out with Euan, since that night with Darcy, but it was the first I hadn't been expecting an ass-kicking. They were still together. Euan had been surprisingly cool about it, which put me hugely on edge at first, until I realised there was just no sucker-punch coming.

The party was loud, and the house was rocking. In fact, the party was too loud, because Euan is a man who likes to show people what his stereo can do. He is also incapable of judging which of his friends will appreciate that sort of thing. We all generally get blasted, first by his unstoppable enthusiasm for new punk and hefty speakers, and then by what feels like a brick wall with a decibel sign after it. The enthusiasm is a good thing, and you can't knock it, but after a few drinks it becomes absolutely unwaning. When we finally got Euan to put the volume down we were able to hear only our own tinnitus. Eventually, people from other houses came round to complain. We couldn't hear them.

There was some smoking going on, Dick showed me a couple of his guitars while he was still sober enough to hold them, and Frank pulled his usual special move – drinking relentlessly in an armchair.

After a while Darcy showed up, and played a fast game of catch up, both with me and with the drink. We chatted and hugged, and things seemed back to normal for the first time in weeks. I watched her canoodling with Euan through my pint glass and didn't really feel anything, other than drunk. It was good to be merely merry again. It was a relief to stop being serious.

Eventually Dick was sick into a bucket in the lounge, and Darcy took over and mothered him for a while, before knocking the bucket over onto her feet and getting half-sick herself, and then passing out in Euan's bedroom. We all left the pungent lounge post-haste, Frank and I to chow on the leftovers of a Chinese carryout in the kitchen.

Somewhere along the way Dick disappeared, too, and when it was time to hit the beach only a handful of us remained, Frank, Euan, and myself, as well as a couple of girls who had broken the rules and changed into swimming costumes.

There was a crowd, a choir, and a piper on the beach. Some people were singing, some were in fancy dress, others were wandering around with confused looks on the faces. It could have been the scene of an eclipse at a village fete, possibly during Oktoberfest. A few brave souls were already splashing about a bit, but most were standing on the beach, idly chatting and watching the horizon.

I hadn't brought a towel, for the second year running. I had gone one better and brought a tatty green full-length dressing gown. I was all for the skinny dipping, but I wasn't going to stand around on the beach afterwards, the intention was to hide my shame as quickly and completely as possible. I didn't much care for people seeing my cock on the way in, but I sure as hell didn't want them to catch a glimpse on the way out.

I changed on the beach in true British form, slipping off my boxer shorts underneath the protective cover of the gown, exposing not one unnecessary inch of flesh. Then I blew my cover completely, by discretely trying to fondle some warmth back into my nether regions. Frank eyed me, distastefully.

'It's the size of a peanut,' I protested. 'How cold is it, already?'

'Don't be a pussy,' he remonstrated. 'You're not here to show off.'

He was right. I definitely was not there to show off. Not my pasty white ass, and not my quickly receding scrotum. I was not there to show off at all. Standing barefoot on the beach, cupping my balls through the soft towel cloth of my dressing gown, staring into the inky black of the north sea, I began to question why exactly I was there.

'This is a fucking laugh, eh?' Frank said.

That was it. It was a laugh.

'I can't feel my dick, anymore,' I shivered.

'You should stop trying,' Euan said, with a frown.

And then it was dawn. It was an amazing thing. I have always been a night owl, and I have seen my fair share of sunrises. I am still amazed by the speed of a dawn. That objects as immense as the sun and earth should relate in human time sends me reeling. Students ran like lemmings into the ocean. Some of them cried out in what could only have been real physical pain.

'I'll hold your towels, guys,' I said, looking down at my cold, cold feet.

Euan and Frank ran into the ocean, too. There was much laughter and splashing. It might as well have been the public baths, as far as they were concerned. Except that, running out of it again, side by side, they were hit by a solid wall of flash photography. I blinked a few times, and handed them their towels.

'That was wicked,' Frank said. 'Are you bottling it, Quinine?'

'No,' I said, lying. 'I just didn't want to be caught on candid camera.'

'That was wicked,' Frank said again. 'I couldn't see a thing. Come on, Quinn – this is your chance to Man Up.'

'I don't give a fuck,' I said, defiantly. But as I said it, I realised that it was true.

Frank looked at me, expectantly.

'Hold my dressing gown,' I said, resignedly calling over my shoulder. 'Make sure it's ready for me when I get back.'

I walked down to the water, striding like the Emperor in his fancy new clothes. I waded in, just waist high at first. The water was like a liquid icepack, but I could feel the sensation being distanced by the alcohol. The worst part was when the water first tickled the hairs on my sack, and I forced myself onto tiptoes, to avoid the inevitable wave of ball-crushing coldness.

Eventually I took the plunge, all at once, in to my shoulders. I was under for a second or two at most, and I drew breath and a little water with the shock. Then I turned around, and ran for the beach, covering myself with both hands, which probably wasn't necessary. As I neared the shore, a small ripple in the sand caught me off balance, and I fell face first into the froth of the breaking waves. I exposed myself to the entire beach, instinctively rubbing the sand out of my eyes, and then pelted over to Frank, who respectfully fitted me with the gown.

'Thanks,' I said, feeling much better.

'Let's get out of here,' he said. 'I'm fucking freezing.'

On the way off the beach, we met Dylan and Joanne, as well as James, one of Dylan's perma-stoned associates. We went back to his room in Sallies and turned on the heating. It was soon pretty warm, and Frank went and took a shower, while I lounged around in my dressing gown. I couldn't get the taste of saltwater out of my mouth, but Dylan rolled a solution, and we smoked it out of the window. It was very laid back and cosy, until Frank returned and starting hurling abuse out of the window at the last stragglers shivering their way along from the beach.

'I'm taking it easy, from now on,' I told Dylan. 'No more gear, no more crazy, no more freezing seawater. No more fucking nudity. No more stupid crushes, no more destruction. No more jumping through hoops. I'm tired, man.'

'No way,' Dylan said. 'No way.'

Maybe he was surprised, or maybe he'd just heard it before. I always do pretend that things are over.

Post

What's to say about the year I spent in Fife Park? I felt like I couldn't be hurt, but I was. I thought I had a plan, but everything was a mess. I thought there was a glow, but it doesn't stand out like a glowing thing should.

It's late in the spring, and I'm thinking of Fife Park. I thought I could pick up the past, and see it as I did then. But I only see it as it seems now; it was just the kind of stupid shit you'd expect a dumb kid to do, and afterwards I grew up.

I had a plan for change that year. And it was ridiculous, I knew it at the time, but I lived like it was true. I didn't change, in the ways I thought I would. I didn't become the person I hoped; I didn't understand what he would be anyway.

But I did random things because they were random. I did serious things because they were serious. And I was too serious about them, and it was funny, and I laughed with myself. I was so in touch with the time, as it went by.

What an idiot idea it was to try and boil that down. The answer is there in the wholeness of it. It can't be condensed for convenience or narrative. What I had then, that I lost, was all of it. It was a whole life, complete and constantly renewing. It was everything I was; that glow burned out of the core of me, and lit up everything I saw.

And so I have retraced my steps to the end. The truth was never anything like I remember it, and what I remember was never a feeling at all: it was a person, and I am what is left.

But I have a picture in my head of Quinn Wilde, that lost idiot youth, that fool nonpareil with the dyed red hair. I didn't think I knew him still, but now I've come to know him better than before. He's a glowing exemplar of all the ways I'd like to be. He is an aspiration. He's pure fiction.

And now he's shed his youth as well. The crows feet suit him well, and his eye-scar crinkles when he smiles. Like a kind of conscience, he made me restless when I threw my joy away. He brought me back, and made me look again. Now I want what he would want, much more than what I have. Now I want to live like him, much more than like myself.

And when I wonder what Quinn Wilde would do, the answer is quick and clear: he'd write a book about Fife Park, and muse about his past, and wonder what he lost, and how he changed, and if he grew.

And he would very definitely want the world to know, and he'd make his book a real thing, and he'd hold it up as if to say, 'I am still here, we are still fine, you always were a worrier.'

And he'd maybe post a copy to you too; if you're lucky enough to live in Fife Park.

Thanks, Acknowledgements and Greetz go to:

Ella Wilde,

John Dylan,

Michael Holmes,

all the good (and entirely fictional) people I have caricatured and maligned in writing this; all the residents of Fife Park past and present; all the *Internet Jerks Extraordinaire* at the Sinner; everybody I blew off (socially) whilst pulling sixty hour weeks so that this would be finished before Fife Park got knocked down; all the lost souls who, having passed the event horizon, never managed to leave St. Andrews; and everyone who recognises a place or feeling in this book. Last, but not least, my brothers:

Mart, Craig, Frank, Gowan, Lance, Zorg and Mush.

To prenders

Fucking hates mushrooms